The Anonymous Hookup

Jax Calder

Copyright © 2022 by Jax Calder

All rights reserved.

No part of this book may be reproduced in any form or by any electronic or mechanical means, including information storage and retrieval systems, without written permission from the author, except for the use of brief quotations in a book review.

This is a work of fiction. Names, characters, places and incidents are either the product of the author's imagination or are used fictitiously, and any resemblance to actual persons, living or dead, business establishments, events or locales is entirely coincidental.

Cover design by R.Bosevski of Story Styling Cover Design.

Also by Jax Calder

Sporting Secrets Series:

Playing Offside: A M/M enemies to lovers sports romance

Playing at Home: A M/M manny romance

Playing for Keeps: A M/M friends to lovers sports romance

Short Stories/Novellas

The Inappropriate Date: a M/M short novella

Coming out at the Ball Game: a sweet YA LGBTQ+ short story

Being Set Up: a M/M short novella

Standalone Romance

The Other Brother: a YA/New Adult M/M romance

Chapter One

"You need to have a hookup," is how my friend Jules first broaches the idea. No lead in, but that's Jules to a tee. Jules has been my best friend since we were ten and she doesn't call a spade a spade. She calls it a poor excuse for a shovel.

"No strings, just hot and heavy sex," she continues as she stirs her cocktail and takes a giant slurp.

"I'm not ready for another boyfriend," I say.

"For an English teacher, you have poor comprehension skills sometimes. I didn't say get laid in the hope it leads to more. I said to get laid, period." Jules' voice gets louder at the end, causing me to dart a glance around the restaurant to make sure no one has overheard us. But all the other patrons seem to be simply enjoying their Saturday night meal rather than eavesdropping on the conversation happening at table eight.

Jules is watching me with her eyebrow raised.

"I've never done the hookup thing before," I hedge.

"Well, it's time you learned. In fact, you know how you offered to do a guest article for my blog? I've just come up with your theme. A beginner's guide to a hookup." She leans back in her seat, grinning the type of triumphant grin I imagine graced Napoleon's face when he became Emperor of France. Or maybe Atilla the Hun's when he did whatever he did to live forever in infamy.

"I was thinking more of a post on the history of Auckland Pride," I say.

"It's been, what, five months since you and Preston broke up?" Jules asks.

Five and a half actually, but I don't volunteer this information. Jules' question had a rhetorical feel anyway.

"And you haven't slept with anyone since, right?"

Jules seems to be successfully conducting this conversation by herself. She doesn't need my input.

"I'm pretty sure Preston is not being as restrained."

Preston is definitely not showing any restraint about moving on, if the photos he's posted on social media are anything to go by. Not that I've checked more than twice. A day. Every day since he left.

Jules' grin has a touch of evil in it now. "In fact, I think you should go even further than just a hookup. You need to have an anonymous hookup. Your blog post can be titled 'A beginner's guide to an Anonymous Hookup.' That way your brain won't invent some fun fairy tale about how the guy is going to morph into your Mr. Right." Jules leans forward, her eyes intent on mine. "See if you can have some hot, wild, steamy sex with someone without exchanging names. I'm talking about sex where it's simply about the mind-blowing orgasms, nothing else. It's time you sowed your wild oats."

One of the reasons why Jules' blog is growing so quickly in popularity is she has the gift of painting a picture with words.

The Anonymous Hookup

Suddenly my mind filled with images of hot, steamy sex. Of another hard body pressed up against mine. Of mouths grappling, hands sliding across skin, the overwhelming pleasure that comes from touching and being touched.

Heat rises up my chest and neck as images swirl in my mind.

Sex. I like sex.

And it has been a long time.

I'm twenty-five. My sex life really shouldn't have boiled down to the quality relationship between my right hand and my laptop.

Luckily Jules fails to sense my arousal. She'd give me endless crap about it, along with using it as evidence that I really, really need to take her advice and get laid.

Instead, she's distracted herself with another line of thought. "Where does that phrase come from anyway? Why oats?"

I blink, trying to catch up with the new lane this conversation has swerved into. "What?"

"I mean, why are wild oats the grain people get to sow? Why not barley? Or wheat? Is there something more sexually promiscuous about oats?"

I groan. "Please stop now while you're so far behind."

She grins. "Okay, but only if you agree that we're going to Thumpers tonight. And the first guy you lay eyes on, you're going to proposition."

I raise my eyebrows. "Proposition?"

"Yep. Just tell him you want to have wild, crazy animal sex with him."

I feel a repeat of a blush coming, so I quickly grab my beer and take a large swallow.

When I set it down, Jules is still waiting expectantly for me to answer.

"Okay," I say.

* * *

I've always thought Thumpers, the most popular gay nightclub in Auckland, is aptly named, because I've never failed to leave without a thumping headache. It might have something to do with the flashing multi-colored lights and the music being played at about twice the recommended volume. Goodbye to the ability to detect high pitched sounds. It was fun while it lasted.

"First guy you see," Jules instructs after we show our ID to the bouncer and make our way into the club. It's ten-thirty, so the place is already pumping.

I tilt an eyebrow skeptically. "First guy I see?"

"First guy you see who you find attractive," she concedes. "I mean it, Lane. No mucking around. You're looking for a hookup, not a life partner. And if the first guy isn't interested, then you just move on to the next one."

"You make it sound so simple."

"It is simple. You're like a younger, better-looking Chris Pratt. Any guy should thank his lucky stars to hook up with you."

I don't have time to respond to her compliment because she's abruptly stopped halfway to the bar. "There. Him. Do you find him attractive?"

I follow the direction of her nod and my mouth goes dry. The guy she's indicated is the dictionary definition of tall, dark and handsome. He's standing at the bar ordering a drink so I can only see his profile, but it's definitely one of the finer profiles I've ever had the good fortune to stare at. Cut jaw, straight nose, full lips.

"Is it actually possible not to find him attractive?" I ask.

"Then you've found your first target."

"Wow, we're using war terminology now, are we?"

She nudges me. "Don't overthink it. Just get over there."

Severely questioning my life choices and taste in friends, I make my way over to the bar.

Jesus. He's even hotter up close. He's leaning up against the bar, sipping at his drink, surveying the club, which gives me a chance to check him out as I approach. Yep, he's definitely tipping the scales toward gorgeous. He's an inch or two taller than my six feet, with thick dark hair, olive skin, and smouldering dark eyes. He looks around my age, maybe a few years older.

Forget dry. The contents of my mouth could now be used as a desiccant.

I try to keep my legs from shaking as I slot into the space next to him and turn to meet those gorgeous eyes.

"Hi," I say.

"Hey," he says, giving me both a charming grin and a quick once over. Which is quite a multi-skilled talent, when you think about it.

"I'm..." I begin, then realize I'm already about to break the rules for an anonymous hookup.

He quirks an eyebrow. "You're what?"

"I'm really thirsty," I say, then almost close my eyes in embarrassment as my cringe reflex hits me.

"Well, that's great. You've definitely come to the right place." Luckily he seems more amused than scornful at my absolute lack of game.

I flick a look at Jules who has settled on a stool at a high table on the other side of the bar. She gives me something between an encouraging nod and a 'do it or else I'll hassle you about how pathetic you are.'

I take a deep breath. "You want to get out of here?"

His brow creases. Yeah, confusion wasn't the response I was going for.

"I thought you said you were thirsty," he says.

"I am." I load those two words with enough innuendo it's surprising they make it out of my mouth.

His confusion lifts and a slow smile spreads across his face. "Oh, that kind of thirsty."

It appears I've chosen my metaphor hill to die on. "Yeah, that kind."

"And you're offering me the chance to help quench your thirst."

"Um...yes I am."

"Well, lucky for you, I consider myself extremely gifted in the art of hydration."

I can't help laughing. He's funny, which definitely helps me to relax. Funny and gorgeous... my brain starts to race off, but I wrench it back with a thud.

"Ah...just so you know, I'm only recently out of a relationship. I'm not looking for anything serious," I say.

His eyebrows shoot up. "You're kidding me, right?"

I blink. "What?"

"Because I was just about to message my ring engraver. He's been on standby for years, just waiting for me to say the name of my beloved."

His face splits into an open grin as he laughs at my reaction.

"Okay." I roll my eyes. "I haven't done the hookup thing before, but I just wanted to make sure we were on the same page."

The Anonymous Hookup

He quirks an eyebrow. "You've never had a hookup before? Seriously?"

"Seriously. My friend thinks it's hilarious. She wants me to write an article for her blog 'A beginner's guide to an anonymous hookup.'"

"Oh, that's brilliant. I'll happily help you with that." He props his arm on the bar as he continues to grin at me.

"So you can't tell me your name," I continue, because sometimes I can't turn off the teacher side of me, which needs to know all the rules have been understood.

"Ooh, I like this idea. Can I use a fake name then?"

"If you want."

He strokes his chin. "I've always fancied myself as a Wilbur. Or maybe Fred? Actually, do you think I can pull off Bernie?"

"Please don't call yourself Bernie. My uncle's name is Bernie."

He slants his eyes at me. "Aren't you worried about telling me that piece of information?"

"I fail to see how knowing my uncle's name is Bernie is going to lead you to discover my real identity."

"If you don't think I can track down every Bernie in New Zealand and closely examine their family tree, you seriously underestimate my skill level."

I can't help laughing again. God, this guy is really something.

He leans in closer to me, and I catch a whiff of his cologne. "And that's the last time you're allowed to underestimate my skill level." His husky voice whispering into my ear and the puff of his breath on my neck triggers my cock, which gives a twitch.

"I promise I won't underestimate your skill level, Fred." My voice comes out slightly breathless.

He pulls back and gives me a heated look. "Right, you're looking parched. I don't want you to expire, so I suggest we move this hydrating exercise to the next stage."

We smile at each other. Then he takes a last swig of his drink and detaches from the bar, leading the way through the crowd.

I follow close behind, my heart racing.

I glance at Jules who wears a massive grin and gives me two thumbs up.

Following him gives me a chance to appreciate him even more. He has broad shoulders but is lean everywhere else, although the cut of his button-down shirt shows he's definitely got some muscles lurking under there.

When we make it out to the pavement, he turns to me. "So, in keeping with the anonymous theme, do you want to get a hotel room?"

"Good idea," I say.

He pats his pocket. "Luckily I came out tonight all prepared like a good boy scout. And I tested negative for all the nasties just last week. I can show you my results if you want."

Shit.

I haven't even thought about that aspect of hooking up.

"I...uh.... I got tested when my relationship ended five months ago. And I haven't been with anyone since."

His eyes twinkle. "That's a long time between drinks. No wonder you're so thirsty."

"Ah...yeah."

I struggle to match his light-hearted banter. Because this conversation has just reinforced what's happening, and one part of me can't believe I'm actually doing this. This is a complete stranger and I'm going to have sex with him.

Something about my expression must make him realize

how outside my comfort zone I am. I'm talking lying on a bed of nails suspended over the Grand Canyon out of my comfort zone.

"Hey." He steps closer to me. "You're not freaking out on me, are you?

This close, with the light shining from a street lamp above, I can see how long his eyelashes are. It's a ridiculous thing to focus on, but somehow it makes me feel better. The universe wouldn't bestow Bambi-eyelashes on someone who wasn't a decent person, right?

I take a deep breath. "I'm not freaking out."

Then I close the remaining distance between us and kiss him.

It seems like a good idea, because if there's no chemistry between us, it's best to find out now.

What happens is the opposite of no chemistry. In fact, there's a whole periodic table of chemistry in this kiss.

His lips are smooth and warm and our kiss deepens so quickly my head spins. Our tongues meet in what is probably the most awesome slide in the history of kissing. He tastes like beer along with something else, something masculine and so, so addictive. One of his palms comes up to touch the side of my face, while my hands have found their way to his hips, pulling him closer to me. His warmth seeps through his shirt where our bodies touch.

I'm panting when we draw apart, staring in disbelief at this gorgeous stranger, who kisses like he's both a god and a devil combined into one.

Thankfully, he appears as affected by the kiss as I am. His dilated pupils are large pools of black and his chest is heaving.

For a few seconds we only stare at each other.

"I think we'd better get that room," he says finally.

"Ah... yeah."

There's a decent hotel right across the street, so we head there as I try to regain my composure.

We have a mild standoff at the reception desk about whose credit card is footing the bill. He tries to hand his over, but I shoulder jostle him out of the way, ignoring the fact that the receptionist is watching us with amusement.

I am not letting the guy I randomly propositioned pay for a hotel room for us to have sex in. It seems to go against the etiquette of random hookups. Not that I'm particularly well acquainted with the rules, but anyway.

Eventually he relents and lets me hand over my credit card. He takes a few steps back and gives me privacy, which I guess helps to maintain the anonymity thing.

He follows me to the elevator and I punch in our floor number.

"Is this the part where you cross-examine me to check I'm not a serial killer?" he asks as we start our ascent.

"Nah, I'm not too worried about that."

He raises an eyebrow. "You're not? Do I not give out proper serial killer vibes?"

"Nah, you don't really. And I was the one who propositioned you, remember?" I meet his gaze in the elevator mirror. "Plus, I think the probability of two serial killers being in the same elevator is extraordinarily low."

His laugh echoes off the walls.

"I stole that off a meme," I admit.

A dimple quirks in his cheek. "That's reassuring. I think I'd prefer you to be a meme stealer rather than a serial killer, although it's a close call."

Our room is opposite the elevator. A quick slide of the key and we're inside. He shuts the door and turns to me. There's still a trace of laughter on his lips, which somehow makes me feel better. Because how do we get this started? Sex in the context of relationships seems to happen organically, but right now I feel stilted and unnatural. We both know what we're here for, but I don't know what my first move should be.

Wanna have sex now? It isn't exactly the most inspiring line ever thought up.

He's studying me, appearing to be waiting for me to say or do something.

I take a deep breath. "So, you're going to help me with my article, right? A beginner's guide to an anonymous hookup. How would you suggest we start?"

A smile edges up his face. "Oh definitely, I'm all about supporting the self-help industry. And in this case, I think you'll find kissing is a good place to begin."

He steps closer to me, and I can feel the frisson of anticipation between us.

"I think I can manage some kissing," I say.

"You proved earlier you're very good at kissing." His dark eyes don't leave mine. "But I feel like I might need some more proof."

I don't move as he closes the gap between us, leaning in.

His mouth is soft against mine, a light brush of lips that feels like a tease.

I have never had such a gentle, sweet kiss, never had the chance to contemplate exactly how many nerve endings are in my lips, and how one simple touch can set my entire body alight.

Our kiss stays light, our lips the only point where we connect. His breath mingles with mine. It's like a Mexican standoff to see who can resist the urge to deepen the kiss first.

Then I feel his tongue lightly probe between my lips

and I give in, groaning as I deepen the kiss urgently. Our kiss ramps up until we're kissing desperately.

One of his hands comes up to cradle my head, threading his fingers through my hair. We stumble back against the wall, our bodies pressing together, and the feeling of his hardening cock against mine makes me moan.

I wrench my mouth away from his, gasping.

"You're definitely right that kissing is a good place to start." My voice is husky as I kiss down his neck. "But you didn't specify exactly where the kissing should be."

I undo the top button of his shirt and press my lips to the sliver of tan skin exposed, wondering where this burst of confidence has come from. I'm running with it though.

He shivers, and that spurs me on to repeat the gesture with the next button, and the next. Shit. The slightly salty taste of his skin, the lingering scent of his cologne, makes my cock throb.

His chest is well defined, but not too Chippendale to make me feel bad about my own physique.

Sliding to my knees, I undo his last button and place a gentle, lingering kiss on his taut stomach. My heart thuds.

I glance up and he's watching me, his eyes dark with lust, his chest rising and falling.

I take that as a sign he's okay for me to fumble his belt buckle with my shaking hands, to undo his button and zipper so his pants fall to puddle around his feet.

His breath hitches as I tug down his boxers.

It turns out his cock is as gorgeous as the rest of him and I lean forward, taking the tip into my mouth.

"Oh fuck." His head lolls back against the wall.

I've never done this before, never been so assertive in a sexual encounter. But there's something confidence inducing about knowing I'm not going to see him again.

Judging by the harshness of his breathing, he's liking this turn of events too.

Moving my mouth down, taking him deeper into my throat, only increases my own throbbing, to the point where I feel like I'm going to explode myself if I continue too long.

I pull off.

He stares down at me, his eyes wrecked, lips swollen from our earlier kisses.

"Fuck," he mutters.

"Is that what you want?" I ask.

Shit. I can't quite believe I'm being this forward, but I'm enjoying being Hookup Lane, who's not worried about any long-term consequences, who's simply focusing on feeling good right here, right now.

His eyes darken with lust. "I guess we should discuss the hard limits here. Besides me saying or doing anything to remind you of your great uncle Bernie."

I huff out a laugh as I get to my feet. "Well, it seems like a shame to waste a perfectly good bed."

"Yeah, it does." His voice is husky. "You're a top, right? Because I think that was the most toppy blow job I've had in my life."

"I'm actually versatile," I say.

"Me too. What do you feel like tonight?"

My eyebrows shoot up at the casualness with which he asks that question.

Shit. It's like the choice between two delicious flavors of ice cream.

That's the problem with a one-night stand, right? In any other circumstance, I wouldn't be too concerned about choosing, because I'd get to experience the other option. But given this is going to be my only experience with him, what do I want more?

"Um…" Damn. I'd never been particularly good at making decisions.

He leans down to rummage in his pants and triumphantly produces a coin. "How about I flip you for it?"

"We're flipping a coin to decide who's fucking who?" I clarify.

"Why not?"

Why not indeed? In fact, 'Why not?' seems to be my motto for the evening.

"Fine."

"You can be heads since we've already discovered you give great head." He flicks a wink at me. "Heads, you do me, tails, I do you."

"Okay."

I'm happy putting this into the hands of the universe. Judging by what has happened so far, I'm going to have a great time either way.

He flips the coin.

"Tails," he says.

Which means he's fucking me.

A shiver shoots down my spine in anticipation.

"Okay. Um…it's been a while, so…uh…"

He seems to find my stumbling endearing, because he gives me a warm smile. "Don't worry, I'm all about prepping. I could be a master sous chef. Or one of those survivalists who prepares for the end of the world."

"Did you seriously compare fucking me to the end of the world?"

He bursts out laughing and I join in.

Shit. I don't think I'd ever had half as much fun during sex as I'm having right now.

But as our laughter fades, he leans forward to kiss me and things go from funny to scorching within a second.

The Anonymous Hookup

We stagger back toward the bed, falling on it in a tangle of arms and legs. He proves himself extremely adept at clothes removal, stripping mine off as he continues to kiss me thoroughly.

His fingers trail down my body leaving goosebumps in their wake.

True to his word, he's incredibly patient at prepping me. Taking his time, one finger then two, carefully stretching me, hooking his fingers inside me and reducing me down to a trembling, heaving mess so when he finally withdraws to put on a condom, I'm ready to combust with want.

My body trembles as he lines himself up.

He watches me carefully as he starts to press inside.

This amount of eye contact feels too intimate, yet I can't break our gazes.

"You okay?" he asks.

I nod wordlessly.

I can read every micro expression on his face as he slowly inches in. Wonder. Pleasure. Awe.

One of his eyebrows is quirked, like there's something about this experience he can't quite figure out.

The pleasure-pain is intense, my nerve endings thrumming.

When he finally bottoms out we both groan.

He brings his lips down to mine in a bruising kiss that somehow gentles to something sweeter as he slowly starts to move.

I hook my legs around him, angling my hips, encouraging him with my body to go harder.

Fuck. He hits the spot inside and stars light up my vision.

"Like that," I gasp. "Again."

He obeys me, propping himself up on his elbows as he pounds out a rhythm that means I'm not only seeing stars, I'm seeing galaxies.

"Feels too good," he grits out. The corded muscles in his neck pulse. "I can't last much longer."

I squeeze a hand between us so I can grab my cock. It's so hard and I'm so close that it only takes a few strokes and my orgasm charges down with a ferocity I can't stop.

"Oh shit, I'm..."

I don't get to finish the sentence before extreme pleasure shoots through me as I come and come.

He's bucking inside me with his own orgasm. His weight is on me, his face buried in my neck, both of our breathing coming in short gasps.

He slowly pulls out of me.

"Holy hell." He collapses on the bed next to me.

"Yeah," I manage. My brain is currently offline, frolicking in a happy meadow where unicorns and other magical creatures exist.

Prostate orgasms. There's nothing better. Pretty sure we could achieve world peace if only more guys got to experience these.

I'm vaguely aware of him getting out of bed and heading to the bathroom.

He comes back with a warm cloth and gives it to me. My hands are still trembling slightly as I clean myself up. I throw the cloth on to the bedside table, then turn to him.

He stares at me, his expression intent. "I promise I won't break the terms of our deal and beg for a repeat or anything, but... like... wow."

I clear my throat. "Yeah."

"It's probably a good idea if you don't go into too much detail in your blog post, because you might set up false

The Anonymous Hookup

expectations of how good hookup sex actually is, and there will be lots of disappointed people out there."

"What, because they all can't have anonymous hookups with you?" I ask.

"No, because they all can't have anonymous hookups like *us*. Seriously, that was insanely good."

Shit, I like how straight up this guy is. No games. No pretenses. After a relationship filled with both, it's so refreshing to be with someone who simply says what's on his mind.

But... I'm doing it already...looking at him like he's a prospect beyond a simple one-night stand.

I scramble to get out of bed.

"That was exactly what I needed," I say.

"Glad I could oblige." He smirks at me. "I'll put thirst quencher on my resume, shall I?"

"I'll happily write you a letter of recommendation."

"Ah, but that would mean I'd know your name." There almost seems to be a trace of wistfulness in his voice.

We stare at each other and, for a few heartbeats, I consider it. I consider opening my mouth and telling him my name, consider asking for his number, consider arranging to meet up again.

But I'm not ready for that. It wouldn't be fair to him to pursue something when I'm not in the right headspace.

"I need to get going," I mumble instead.

"Please tell me you don't have a wife and seven kids waiting at home for you."

"Definitely not."

I tug my clothes on, trying not to feel bereft. This is what we were here for. The experience has been completed to mutual satisfaction. I shouldn't feel disappointed that it's ending.

He props himself on one elbow and watches me as I get dressed.

And this is the moment where I wish I knew him better, where I wish I could read the expression in his dark eyes. I drop my gaze away from his, but it only lands on his gorgeous chest, which reminds me of how it felt to kiss his skin. It doesn't help to firm up my resolution to keep this as an anonymous hookup, so I relocate my gaze to the floor.

Once I'm fully dressed, I hesitate, because I can't just leave, can I? It feels wrong given what we experienced together.

Before I can second question myself, I take the few steps toward the bed and bend down to kiss him.

I keep it light because I know if I fall into one of his scorching kisses, I'll keep on falling right back into bed.

And I get the feeling if we went another round, I'd break my vow to keep this anonymous. Then where would I be?

It's a sweet kiss. Almost too sweet for the circumstances. Enough. I stumble back.

"Ah... see you around," I say, and then cringe. The whole point of an anonymous hookup is the fact I won't see him again.

Luckily he lets my comment go unchecked.

"See you," he replies.

* * *

I don't have a wife and seven kids waiting at home, but I do have a cocker spaniel called Casper who greets me with a thumping tail.

I lucked into this house-sitting arrangement just as Preston and I broke up, and it saved me from having to wrestle with the dire Auckland housing market. Casper's owners are overseas for a year, and in exchange for a free place to live, I only have to look after Casper and the grounds of their beautiful Grey Lynn villa. It's worked out great so far. Casper is a fantastic roommate once you get past the excess slobber that he shares freely.

While he's outside doing his business, I send Jules a message.

Anonymous hookup achieved.

I accompany my message with lots of smiley faces.

She sends me back a smiley face and an eggplant emoji.

I huff out a laugh.

I feel pretty good about the whole thing. I proved I can mix it up, I can go outside my comfort zone, have scorching hot sex without any strings. Another life skill mastered.

And for once, when I check Instagram, photos of Preston out having a good time fail to cause my stomach to hollow.

Because I had a great night too.

And instead of falling asleep thinking about Preston and all the ways our relationship went wrong, I drift off to sleep remembering a dark haired, dark eyed guy who kisses better than anyone I could ever dream up.

Chapter Two

The afterglow of great sex lasts me through all of Sunday and even Monday, when I'm back at work trying to get teenagers to care about active and passive verbs.

At lunchtime when I check my email it appears life has continued its theme of rewarding me.

"Yes!" I do a fist pump my students would mock me endlessly for. Luckily I'm in my office, with only my colleague Errol to raise a bushy eyebrow at my antics.

"That's far too enthusiastic for a Monday," he says.

"I got an email saying that we got selected into that TV mentorship program I told you about!" I can't keep the excitement from my voice.

Errol's cynical smile is replaced with a real one. "That's awesome news."

The school we work at in South Auckland has lots of students from disadvantaged backgrounds, and I'm determined to make sure they get offered every opportunity possible.

So when I'd heard about a project where some of New

Zealand's best TV directors were going to work with groups of students for a year's mentorship, I'd put some of my most talented students forward for the opportunity.

My Year 12 class had worked hard on their audition video, and I'd ignored rumors our nearest private school had hired a professional production company to make theirs.

We were used to being David in his battle against Goliath.

And I can't help feeling triumphant now, especially when I scan the email again and see the other two schools selected are private schools from the North Shore.

Preston's voice makes an unwelcome entry into my head. *"Why the hell are you wasting your time teaching? You're a smart guy. You could earn so much more if you got a proper job."*

Preston is an accountant, so money is an important focus in his life. I can't completely blame him. Auckland is one of the most unaffordable cities in the world and the cost of living seems to go up every month. I'm so lucky my house-sitting arrangement means I can save some of my meagre teacher's income toward a house deposit, but it still looks like a daunting task to get on the property ladder.

I always felt Preston had counted that against me, knowing if he was with me long- term I could never contribute much to the glittering lifestyle he wanted.

For a second, I have an urge to forward the email about the mentorship to Preston with a note across the top.

This is why I teach, Preston. Because some things are more important than money.

Instead, I hit reply and email Claire, the coordinator, back.

Thank you so much for this! It has made my day. My students are going to be so excited when I tell them the news.

Only a minute later, Claire's reply pings into my inbox.

You're very welcome. The committee loved your audition tape. I'm going to ask your students for advice if I ever want to propose to anyone.

I laugh, because instead of doing a serious audition video about world issues, we'd come up with the idea of giving advice on how to propose to someone, along with acting out some scenarios.

I'm glad it was a hit. And I'm sure my students will be willing to help you out... for a small fee, of course.

Claire's reply comes back almost immediately.

Of course. I wouldn't expect to get that standard of help without some form of payment. By the way, this just popped up on my social media feed and I thought you could show it to your students.

I click on the link she sent me and watch a flash mob proposal under the Eiffel Tower. It makes me smile.

"You're still far too happy for a Monday," Errol complains.

* * *

With all the excitement about getting a place in the mentorship program and meeting with my students after last period to tell them about it, I'm late leaving school. In Auckland, this means an epic battle with traffic.

I usually aim to get to Casper's doggie daycare by four thirty to miss the rush, but today it's after five by the time I make it. I wait patiently as the staff bustle around trying to reunite owners with their dogs.

Erin, a small woman in her fifties who has dog controlling superpowers, collects Casper for me while I wait outside the gate to the main play enclosure. They have air fresheners strategically placed around the entrance area, but nothing can mask the overall doggie smell.

"He had a great day," Erin tells me when she re-emerges, Casper tugging on the lead. "Boris has been here today, and so the two of them played all day as usual."

I feel like a proud parent hearing their child made a friend in the playground. Casper can be quite timid around other dogs, but apparently Boris the German Shepherd cross always brings out his more confident and sociable side.

"That's great. He's always so tired after a day playing with Boris," I say.

"Oh, here's Boris's owner now." Erin looks over my shoulder.

I turn around, the smile on my lips freezing when I meet a pair of dark eyes.

Familiar dark eyes.

Familiar dark eyes that widen in shock.

He stops abruptly, his forehead creasing.

My anonymous hookup is wearing a sharp suit with a blue shirt and he's got more stubble than he had on Saturday night. It suits him.

My breath leaves me. I'm not sure if it's simple shock, or if my lungs are also distracted by clocking how good he looks and forgetting about their essential function of getting oxygen into my body.

"This is Casper and Casper's dad," Erin informs him as he stares at me, seemingly dumbstruck. "I was just saying that Boris and Casper spent all day playing together again."

"Oh...right," he says, blinking rapidly.

He still looks flummoxed. I know the feeling.

"I honestly don't think we have two other dogs who like each other as much as Boris and Casper do." Erin gives

Casper a pat on the head as he looks up adoringly at her. "You guys should arrange a play date for them sometime."

She looks expectantly at us.

"A play date..." Boris's dad, aka my anonymous hookup, says like it's a foreign term he doesn't comprehend.

"For the dogs," Erin says encouragingly.

He meets my eyes, quirking an eyebrow. For a moment, I remember that same quirk when he was inside me and my cheeks heat.

I'm not sure if it's embarrassment or arousal. I'm hoping for embarrassment because arousal feels slightly inappropriate given the circumstances.

"Well, I do pride myself on being a good dog owner," he says slowly as he gets out his phone from his pocket.

My heart pounds.

Erin hands Casper's lead to me.

"I'll just grab Boris," she says as she disappears back into the enclosure.

I bend down to make a fuss over Casper, who greets me with a lick to the side of my face. I pat his silky head as I try to compose myself. What should I say? It was supposed to be an anonymous hookup, but I can't deny the idea of seeing him again is incredibly appealing.

When I look up from Casper, he's leaning up against the wall, one side of his mouth twitching up as he regards me.

"So, Casper's dad, do you want to give me your number to arrange the doggie play date we're apparently having?"

I straighten up. "You want my number?"

"I don't want to disappoint Erin and end up in doggie daycare purgatory," he says.

I tilt an eyebrow. "What does doggie daycare purgatory look like?"

"I'm thinking there would be lots of barking dogs," he says in a low voice.

I laugh and his expression lightens.

"So, your number?"

I swallow. Then, taking a deep breath, I rattle it off.

He keeps his eyes on his screen as he inputs it, then types out a message. My phone in my pocket vibrates.

"And now you have my number," he says.

"Great."

Our eyes meet again, and there's so much heat in our gazes, it's a miracle the air between us doesn't combust.

Erin comes back with Boris then, handing his lead over to my anonymous hookup.

"Before I forget, I'll grab the information on the SPCA fundraiser I was telling you about," Erin says to him.

"Oh, that would be great."

Erin scurries away and returns a few seconds later with a sheet of paper.

He folds the paper Erin hands to him carefully into his pocket. Then Casper lunges toward Boris and suddenly there's a tangle of leads that we unsuccessfully try to unravel before Erin takes pity on us and sorts it out herself.

Even after they're untangled, Casper's still straining on his lead trying to get to Boris, his tongue hanging out eagerly. I have to keep hauling him back as we walk out together.

When we reach the car park, Boris's dad turns to me.

"So, contact me if you want to arrange that play date," he says.

I get the subtext. I was the one who insisted on Saturday night that it was a onetime thing. He's putting the ball firmly in my court, letting me know it's my decision if I want to meet again.

"Okay," I say.

It's not until I'm out in the car with Casper secured safely in his travelling cage that I open the message from him.

Hey Casper's owner, this is my number.

P.S. You give great head.

I burst out laughing. And I save the number under 'Boris's owner' in my phone.

I now have to decide whether I'm going to use it.

Chapter Three

All week long, his number sits in my phone like an unexploded grenade.

I put Casper into doggie daycare on Wednesday, and despite my efforts to delay myself by marking essays at school, to 'accidentally' time my arrival at doggie daycare after five o'clock, I don't run into Boris's owner again.

So it looks like I'm just going to have to make a decision based on everything I already know.

I think about his dark eyes and full lips and incredible body and amazing kisses...

And okay, I'm not looking for a relationship right now and he understands that. He'll realize that if anything further happens with us, it will be under the concept of 'play' rather than 'date'.

I can do this right? I mean, I handled the concept of an anonymous hookup, despite having never had one before. I can handle extending the anonymous hookup to another encounter or two, surely?

On Friday last period, I dissect the *Dead Poet's Society's* theme of living life to the fullest with my Year 12 class, and something must sink into my consciousness because when I get home from school, I cave.

Hey Boris's owner, was wondering if you want a doggie playdate sometime this weekend?

I hold my breath as I press send.

His reply comes back almost immediately.

You've got it wrong, I'm actually owned by Boris, not the other way around.

I laugh. I can see the dots bobbing indicating he's writing another message. I wait, drumming my fingers on my leg.

I've consulted Boris and he's definitely keen for a play date. When do you think Casper is likely to be at his most playful?

My heart starts to thud. I'm pretty sure there is a double meaning going on in his message.

Does Saturday afternoon suit? 3ish?

Sure. It's a ... play date.

I grin at that.

My smile fades as I realize we still have to arrange where to meet up. I can't really suggest a hotel as a suitable playdate venue for our dogs, can I?

It feels weird inviting someone to my house when I don't even know his name.

But Doggie Daycare Erin knows him and obviously likes him. He's helping her out with a SPCA fundraiser. All my gut instincts point to the fact he's a decent guy.

Before I can second question myself, I send him my address.

. . .

My certainty fades the next day, and just before three I pace around my living room. What am I doing?

Am I being presumptuous, anyway? There's nothing to say that he's not coming here purely for Boris's entertainment.

Surely we're not going to fall into bed like we've never left it?

Although if I believe that, why the hell did I just have an extraordinarily long shower that involved some extremely thorough washing?

Hey, personal hygiene is a good concept. Everyone should practice it.

To settle my scattered thoughts, I grab my phone and check my latest game of chess. I started playing online chess while I was at university as a way to destress myself, and I've kept up the habit since I started teaching.

I have a few regulars I like to play against, but my favorite is Charles Dickens.

And while I'd quite like to pretend I'm playing the ghost of a literature icon, I'm pretty sure the real Dickens wouldn't have been so expressive in his trash talking about my chess moves. Like right now, after I move my knight into an attacking position against his queen, a comment pops up on my screen.

Charles Dickens: *You call that a move?*

ChessLover 365: *I'm lacking any other words to describe it, so yes, that is my move.*

Charles Dickens: *Cue my evil laugh. Because you just walked into my trap.*

He moves his queen to D7, so it's loitering near my rook, but I've spotted a flaw in his strategy. I quickly move my queen to where he's left his bishop unprotected, taking the piece.

ChessLover 365: *Was leaving your bishop exposed to my queen part of your trap?*

Charles Dickens: *All part of my master plan, Padawan.*

ChessLover 365: *Are we doing Star Wars' references now? I'm looking forward to seeing what your Jedi mind tricks can accomplish against me.*

Charles Dickens: *Sadly, you have remained impervious to my mind control attempts. Which leaves me to believe you have no mind.*

I snort with laughter as I log out of the app. No doubt when I log back in, I'll have lost a capital piece and have more comments insulting my intelligence and possibly my parentage. It's all part of the fun.

I put my phone down on my coffee table just as there's a knock at my door.

Wiping my sweaty hands on my shorts, I open the door.

Damn.

I've seen him dressed up for a night out and then in a work suit, but I think this – casual jeans, tight grey T-shirt – might be my favorite look on him so far. He looks good enough to lick. Boris sits obediently at his feet.

"Hey," he says.

"Hi," I reply.

For a few moments we stare at each other.

"Are you going to invite us in?" he asks. "Or did you envision this play date was going to take place on your front doorstep?"

My face heats.

"Sorry... sure. Come in."

He and Boris follow me down the hallway to the living area. Casper bounds over and he and Boris greet each other with some mutual sniffing. My anonymous hookup watches them with a cute smile on his face. "I always envy dogs for their upfront way of greeting each other."

I raise my eyebrows. "You want to sniff people in greeting?"

"It would definitely short-cut some things, don't you think?" His eyes crinkle. "You've got nothing to worry about. You'd definitely pass muster if we moved to sniffing as a form of greeting."

"I'm pretty sure that's the most bizarre compliment I've ever been paid," I say.

He laughs. Then his forehead creases. "Now I'm trying to think of the weirdest compliment I've ever had. Someone once told me they liked my earlobes, which was pretty random."

My eyes flick up to his very standard earlobes. Which is a good thing in my opinion. I don't know if anyone wants to have earlobes outside the normal spectrum.

"Your earlobes are very...lobey."

He laughs his deep chuckle and I smile. Shit. I could listen to his laugh all day.

He looks around the living room, taking in the expensive furnishings and ornate Turkish rug.

"This is a nice place you've got here," he says.

"It's not mine." My voice comes out slightly sharper than I intended. "I'm just house-sitting."

I don't want to him to think I'm something I'm not. I couldn't ever afford to live in a place like this.

"Nice place to house-sit then. You're obviously very trustworthy," he says.

My shoulders relax. "I am incredibly trustworthy."

"Besides stealing memes," he says.

"Stealing memes is my only vice," I agree.

While we've been talking, Casper and Boris have

started playing together on the rug in the middle of the living room. Boris's tail thumps against the side of the coffee table.

"Shall we put the dogs outside to play?" he suggests.

"Ah...that's a good idea."

I open the French doors and grab Casper's collar to herd him outside. Boris trots happily along behind.

As soon as they're on the lawn they play tug of war with Casper's rope toy.

We stand side by side on the patio watching the dogs. My skin prickles, like I've got special receptors in my skin tuned only to him. My mind swirls.

What should I say to progress things? What if he's simply here for our dogs to play with each other?

I turn to look at him. He mirrors my body movement, raising an eyebrow expectantly at me.

"You want a drink?" I blurt out.

"You know how much I'm in favor of good hydration." His grin is so hot I'll need to gulp many glasses of water to cool myself.

Lust surges through me.

Holy fuck, I want him so much.

He follows me into the kitchen where I go to the fridge and get glasses of iced water for us.

I carefully set his glass on the breakfast bar. He's watching me closely as I take a gulp of my own drink. He seems to pay particular attention to my throat as I swallow.

"So, what are we going to do while our dogs play?" he asks, his deep voice layered with heat.

Okay, this is ridiculous. I'm single. He's obviously single. We've slept together before. We already know our sexual chemistry is off the charts.

I put my glass down and stalk around the breakfast bar to him.

He watches me with hungry eyes.

"I was thinking something along the lines of this," I say, as I grab his waist and tug him toward me.

His breath puffs out as he rests his hands lightly on my hips.

Anticipation builds between us until I can't bear it anymore and I stretch up to kiss him. There is no gentle lead in to our kiss this time. I kiss him forcefully, and he kisses me back just as greedily.

We stagger to the couch, kissing the entire time. It appears we've discovered some kind of superglue, so when our lips touch, they can't be prised apart.

Because I don't think I've ever been kissed like this. Like I'm something he cannot be without for another moment.

He pulls away from me for a second, looking dazed. "You have witchcraft in your lips," he whispers.

My lungs empty in disbelief. "Did you seriously quote Shakespeare to me?"

His eyebrows shoot up. "You know Shakespeare?"

I roll my eyes. "I might have heard of him."

"I mean, you know that quote?"

"Yes, I know that quote. I'm not sure if I'm up to role-playing Henry V right now though."

He laughs and holy hell, along with the lust that's overtaken my body, I can't help a flash of... like... shooting through me. A handsome, sexy guy who makes me laugh and can quote Shakespeare? It's as if someone has reached into my head and pulled out my ultimate fantasy.

But we're not here to figure out whether he's my fantasy guy or not. We're here to get off.

I kiss him again, my lips already feeling bruised by his relentless kisses.

Then I break our kiss to move my lips down his neck and he groans.

With the memory of our conversation earlier fresh in my mind, I suck lightly on his earlobe, then nip at it teasingly with my teeth, causing him to moan loudly.

He pulls away to stare at me, his pupils dilated.

"Earlobes are my best feature, right?" he says hoarsely.

"They're incredible," I whisper back.

What's incredible is how this feels.

We strip down so fast it's like we're trying to set a record for clothes removal.

He's so gorgeous and I can't resist running my hands everywhere I can over his body. Along the broad planes of his shoulders, the smooth glide of muscles in his back. His skin is warm and smooth and alive beneath my hands.

Meanwhile we continue to kiss and kiss.

I keep thinking of progressing it to actual fucking, because seeing his ass in those jeans was incredibly inspirational, but somehow the kissing and grinding feels so amazing that all thoughts of anything else flee my mind. This is enough. The feel of his lips on mine, his tongue in my mouth, his cock rubbing against mine. It's enough to get me so close, so quickly.

He puts a hand around our cocks and jerks us off together within a minute until my balls clench.

"I'm going to..."

He pulls back to watch my face as I fly over the edge.

"Oh shit," he puffs, and then he joins me.

I come off my orgasmic high and realize we're completely wrapped up in each other, our legs intertwined, stickiness between us, his forehead resting against mine.

Shit. This feels slightly too intimate for the fact we hardly know each other.

"Okay, so that was definitely proof that last weekend wasn't a fluke," he says, his breath against my collarbone.

"Did you think it was a fluke?"

"Well, there was always a chance that a sex god up in heaven decided to send a lightning bolt down to room 243 at the Mariot Hotel."

"Or that room has been blessed as a shrine to good sex by Mother Nature and everyone in that room will always have fantastic hookups," I offer.

He laughs. We're still so close I feel the vibrations of his chuckle through my skin.

He slowly pulls himself up into a sitting position, grabs a box of tissues from the coffee table and cleans himself up.

I manage to make my limbs work and sit up next to him, trying not to feel awkward as I clean myself up and retrieve my boxers from the floor.

He throws the tissues onto the coffee table and then turns to me. "So, have you written the article for your friend's blog yet?"

"No, I haven't."

"I'm guessing this means you might have to change the name of it?" he says. "A beginners' guide to two anonymous hookups when you know the names of each other's dogs?"

I rub at my forehead. "It's definitely getting quite wordy."

"Or you could leave the definition loose," he suggests. I can tell he's trying to keep his voice casual. "A beginners' guide to an extended hookup where we get together anytime both of us feel like mind-blowing sex."

I arch an eyebrow. "Mind-blowing, huh?"

He trails his fingers down my arm, sending sparks of

desire through me despite my recent orgasm. "Well, we're two for two so far, so I'm figuring there's a pattern emerging. And unlike you, I actually have had other hookups, so I have something to measure it by."

My mind swirls. I still haven't responded to the suggestion we continue this.

I can't deny I want him again.

Preston enters my head. How it was good at the start with him too.

And okay, maybe the sex wasn't quite as spectacular and he didn't make me laugh nearly as much, but still, I was convinced that it was a great thing. And look how it turned out.

"I'm still not looking for a relationship," I say, aware there's a note of regret in my voice.

He stares at me for a few heartbeats. "Don't worry, I'm totally onboard for keeping this casual. We can even continue to keep it anonymous if you want."

I snort. "You seriously want to keep things anonymous?"

He leans forward to nuzzle my neck. "It's kind of hot actually, not knowing each other's names," he murmurs in my ear.

Maybe keeping it anonymous is what I need to stop myself from getting too attached. To keep it strictly about the sex, nothing else.

"Okay," I say.

His eyes sparkle as he pulls back, grinning at me. "As long as you don't call me Boris's dad in the bedroom, we're all good."

"It's a deal."

And we seal the deal with another scorching kiss.

Chapter Four

I wait for Jules at a cafe, checking my emails at the same time as I make a few chess moves in my newest game against Charles Dickens. Who says men can't multi-task?

I can't help laughing because Charles Dickens does the same sequence of opening moves in every game and no matter how I respond, he doesn't vary it.

Chesslover365: *Gee, that looks original.*

Charles Dickens: *Originality is my middle name.*

Chesslover365: *Actually your middle names were John Huffam.*

Charles Dickens: *I'm semi-impressed you knew that.*

Chesslover365: *Only semi-impressed???? What do I have to do to impress you??*

Charles Dickens: *I'll tell you when it happens. It's definitely not the fact you just left your knight exposed with that move.*

Shit. He's right.

Okay, so there might be a reason he sticks with that opening sequence of moves. It's fairly effective.

After Charles Dickens takes my knight, I move my bishop to take a pawn in reply. Not a fair trade, but it's the best I can salvage.

I'm waiting for Charles Dickens's return move when my phone beeps with a message. My pulse increases when I see it's from Boris's dad.

Boris is a bit restless today. I really feel like he needs some play time.

I grin as I type my reply.

I wouldn't want to deprive Boris of his play time. I couldn't live with the guilt.

His reply pings back moments later.

You want to come over here? It's my turn to host.

And then he sends me a google map link to his address.

I stare at it. He lives in Mission Bay, one of Auckland's most expensive suburbs. My stomach hollows. I'm not sure if it's because of the confirmation that he's way out of my league, or because he knows where I live and now I know where he lives, which feels like yet more nails in the anonymity coffin.

I quickly tap out a reply.

I'm looking forward to experiencing your hospitality.

His reply comes almost immediately.

Oh baby, you know how much dirty talk does it for me.

I chuckle.

"Ooh... who are you messaging with that grin on your face?" Jules says, dropping a pile of shopping bags at her feet as she sits.

I put my phone down guiltily. "Um... you know that guy I had an anonymous hookup with the other weekend?"

Jules blinks. Then she starts to laugh. "I knew you couldn't do the anonymous hookup thing."

"No, we totally did. I completely rocked that assignment." I'm slightly affronted she doesn't give me credit that I could follow the rules. I totally followed them!

She raises an eyebrow. "So if you managed to keep it anonymous, how are you messaging him?"

"Well...it turns out his dog goes to doggie daycare with Casper."

Jules smirks. "Ha, that's New Zealand for you."

"Yeah, and apparently his dog and Casper love playing together. So we had a playdate for the dogs."

"A playdate for your dogs?" Jules manages to inject cynicism into every word in that sentence.

"Okay, *we* might have done some playing too." My face heats. "But he's happy to keep it as an extended anonymous hookup," I add. "It's only a bit of fun."

Her skeptical expression doesn't change.

"Why are you looking at me like that?" I demand.

"Because I know you." She grabs a menu and scans it.

"What do you think you know about me?"

She raises her eyes from the menu. "You don't do fun."

"Thanks, best friend. That's exactly what everyone wants to hear about themselves."

"You know what I mean. When it comes to relationships, you're usually planning your wedding ceremony halfway through the first date."

"Well, maybe it's time for me to try something different."

Jules puts down the menu, a sympathetic look on her face. "Preston really did a number on you, didn't he?"

My breath rushes out of my lungs and I fiddle with a fork for a few seconds before I answer. "If by that you mean he made me feel inadequate and clingy and has me wondering if I'm cut out for relationships, then yeah, I guess you could say he did a number on me."

"I never liked that pretentious dickhead," Jules says darkly.

"Yeah, I know. You didn't hide that fact very well. You know, that time you said it to his face."

"In my defense, I was drunk."

I raise my eyebrow. "I'm fairly sure half a glass of wine doesn't even put you on the tiddly scale."

"I had alcohol in my system, so therefore the defense stands." She waves her hand dismissively. "Anyway, when do I get to meet your new guy?"

I adjust my voice to patience mode. Luckily, I've had lots of practice with it trying to explain apostrophes to my Year Nine class. "He's my anonymous hookup. We're not meeting each other's friends."

"For now," Jules replies with a smug grin.

* * *

When I arrive at his house that afternoon, I'm determined to prove Jules wrong.

I can do this. Extended anonymous hookup where we know the names of each other's dogs. I mean, how hard can it be?

I clip Casper's leash onto him and get out of the car. He tugs eagerly, his doggie face split into a smile like he knows exactly who he's about to see.

As I take in the house in front of me, I feel my spirits slide. Part of me was hoping to find his house was a shack surrounded by nice houses.

Although let's face it, even a hovel on this street would be worth more than two million. Never mind what the tidy bungalow in front of me is worth.

If he can afford to live here, it means he does well for

himself. He's probably some corporate type who leads a lifestyle I could never keep up with.

But I shouldn't be worried about that for an anonymous hookup. We're not dating. I don't have to keep up with his lifestyle. I only have to keep up with him in bed.

Less than ten minutes later, we're in his bed and I'm doing everything I can to keep up with him, although it's hard because this is definitely an arena he's extremely talented in.

His mouth around my cock is probably the best combination of heat and suction in the history of the planet.

And of course, because I'm all about the giving as well as the receiving, as soon as I come, I shuffle down the bed to return the favor, bringing my A-game, teasing and sucking and doing some tongue work on his head that has him moaning loudly as he comes down my throat.

"Holy hell," he says as I shuffle back up and collapse on the pillow next to him.

"Yeah. Although I'd go more for Holy heaven," I say.

He grins at me. "Holy heaven makes a whole lot more sense when you're talking about blow jobs."

"I agree," I say as he reaches out to stroke my arm, drawing lazy swirls on my skin.

I love how tactile he is after we hook up. Preston was the opposite. He'd almost push me away after he orgasmed. It was after sex he first mentioned the word clingy.

Don't think about Preston.

Taking a deep breath, I glance across and realize he's watching me with his dark eyes.

"Where did you go?" he asks quietly.

I blink. "What?"

"Just now. You looked all blissed out, and then it was like a dark cloud covered your face."

My heart speeds up. Shit. I didn't realize he could read me so well already.

"It's nothing," I say as I sit up. "Guess we better go see what those dogs are up to."

"Yeah, okay." He still has a slightly troubled look on his face as we get out of bed.

I try not to play detective as we walk through his house.

My place is probably easier in keeping up the anonymity thing, because there's not much there that is actually mine.

But his house is different. I see he likes photography from the stunning black and white prints that line his hallway.

And when we reach his living room, his bookcase beckons me like a celestial light.

I pry a familiar friend off the shelf, turning to him with a smile.

"I love *Life of Pi*. I use it to ..." I trail off because I realize he doesn't know I'm a teacher.

He gives me a curious look. "To what? Pray tell, what do you use *Life of Pi* for? As a doorstop? Or as a cure for insomnia?"

"I use it as a comfort read," I say. "It's one of my favorite novels."

I actually use it to teach metaphors but explaining that would mean telling him I'm a teacher. Which is another step toward the anonymous thing not being quite so anonymous.

I keep scanning his bookshelf, pulling out any that catch my interest. Lots of literary classics, sprinkled in among some popular novels and genre fiction. It's a quirky, eclectic collection where Ernest Hemingway rubs shoulders with

Dan Brown. It appears his bookcase is all about the stories he loves rather than about impressing anyone.

"Oh, you've got *The Great Gatsby!* This is my favorite classical novel."

He smiles at me. "I love it too."

I once saw a meme that said seeing someone reading your favorite book was seeing a book recommending a person. I now have an overwhelming number of books recommending him to me.

I could fall in love with the guy for his bookcase alone.

The thought stops me short.

This is not supposed to be about falling in love. Falling in love is not on the agenda. It's not even adjacent to the agenda.

"So, you're a bit of a bibliophile," he says. I look over to see he's watching me, a small smile on his face.

"Ah yeah, you could say that." I guiltily put *Wolf Hall* back in its place. "You obviously are too."

"Yeah, my mum's a literature nut so I couldn't avoid it."

"No one else in my family are big readers, but it's always been my way to escape reality, you know?"

He tilts his head at me. "What are some more of your favorites?"

"*The Road, White Teeth, The Book Thief...* I don't know, it's so hard to choose."

"I love *The Road*. So sparsely written," he says.

"Yeah, it's beautiful. Bleak, but beautiful."

And so we discuss books, discovering all the places where our tastes overlap, and I end up jotting down his recommendations on my phone.

He glances out into the backyard. "The dogs are still playing. Do you want to stay for dinner?"

"Sure." The word is out of my mouth before I think about it.

It's only after I follow him into his kitchen and he starts to rummage in his fridge that I doubt myself.

Should your Extended Anonymous hookup cook you dinner? I'm pretty sure even Siri wouldn't know the answer to that. Although Jules might have an opinion.

We both have to eat, right? It's a basic human function and me staying here for dinner just means we're using our recovery time wisely, and we'll be able to fit in another round of good sex before I go home

Damn, I know Jules has succeeded in getting in my head when I find myself justifying things to her when she's not even here.

I lean forward with my elbows on the breakfast bar as he chops vegetables. "So, what are you cooking me?"

"I was thinking maybe pasta?"

"Sounds good."

"Is Casper okay with having some of Boris's food? It's only biscuits."

"Yeah, that should be fine," I say distractedly, because I've just seen some familiar items pinned to the wall on the far side of his kitchen.

I wander over to examine the medals hanging on multi-colored ribbons, before whirling around to face him. "You run half-marathons?"

He straightens up from where he's retrieved a pot from the cupboard. "Yeah, I do."

"I did the Coatesville and the Waterfront too," I say.

His eyebrows fly up. "Really?"

"Yeah."

How random is it we'd both been in the same place twice in the last few months? I might have jostled for position at the starting line with him, or passed him, or he could have passed me.

"I'm training for the Devonport half-marathon at the moment," he says.

"Me too."

He sets the pot on the stovetop, then raises his gaze to mine. "My training partner has just twisted her ankle. You want to go for a run together sometime?"

"I was planning to go for a training run sometime this weekend," I say.

"How about we go for a run together tomorrow morning?"

My heart pounds like we've already started running. But there's nothing wrong with running together, is there? It's always nicer to run with someone else.

"As long as we get to shower together afterwards." I give him a wink to remind us both what this is all about.

He gives me a lewd wink in return, and I try to outdo him by giving an even more exaggerated wink that almost sprains my eyelid and then he does an even worse one that could double as a face spasm. Then we're laughing, which leads to kissing and heading back to bed where we do all kinds of other fun stuff.

Which makes dinner much later than planned, so by the time we finally eat and clean up it's close to 9pm.

"Casper and I had better get home before we turn into pumpkins," I say afterwards, staring at where Casper is curled up comfortably next to Boris on the couch.

"Stay," he says, reaching out and reeling me into him. His hand brushes under my T-shirt, skimming my back lightly. "Then we can go for a run first thing in the morning."

When he puts it like that, it makes practical sense.

So I fall asleep curled up next to him, his arm draped over my waist, trying desperately not to think about how good this feels.

* * *

Next morning, after a quick dash to my place to grab gear, we run up Mt Eden together.

We stand at the summit looking out at the city of Auckland, to the Sky Tower and to the harbor, Rangitoto Island in the distance.

"It's stunning," I say.

"Yeah," he agrees.

I guess he's used to the view, because when I glance back at him, he's not looking at the expansive city and sparkling water. He's staring at me instead.

We run down and by the time we make it to his house, we're both sweaty messes.

In the interests of water conservation, we shower together, which leads to some spectacular shower sex. Because it appears there's no other variety of sex we can have. This time I finally get to fuck him and having him braced against the shower wall while I thrust inside him is definitely one for my life's highlight reel.

"So...I guess I better get going..." I say as we get dressed.

He grabs a pair of boxers from his top drawer and puts them on. His damp hair is curling slightly and his jaw is rough with stubble. The unshaven look suits him. He's gorgeous and sexy, but he's also so damn cute.

"Any exciting plans for the rest of your day?" he asks.

I wrench my mind away from admiring him to answer. "Nothing exciting. Just mowing the lawns and doing some gardening. It's part of the house-sitting agreement that I keep on top of all of that stuff."

His eyes light up. "Do you know anything about gardening?"

"Um... a bit. My family owns a landscaping business, so they forced me to learn. I enjoy gardening more than mowing lawns. You would not believe the number of lawns I had to mow growing up."

It's only after the words have left my mouth that I realize telling him about my family's business might blur the edges of the anonymous thing.

He tugs on his T-shirt and I try not to mourn the loss of the sight of his chest, but when he looks at me, his eyes are bright. "Oh wow, I really need your help. I only bought this place six months ago, and the back garden is a mess. I don't know where to start."

"I can take a look," I offer.

"Tell you what, I'm great at mowing lawns. We could do a trade. If you give me some advice for my garden, I'll mow your lawns this afternoon."

I hesitate for a second, because this feels slightly outside the boundaries of an extended anonymous hookup. But then, so was running together. And I can't deny that the chance to spend more time with him is infinitely appealing. Plus, there's the fact I really do loathe mowing lawns.

"Sounds like a deal," I say.

So we take a walk around his backyard. It's not that large, but it's got a strip of lawn and some trees to provide the basic structure. However, it's obvious the last owners let it go wild. I make some suggestions about what plants he should keep and what he should remove.

"This place has so much potential," I say as we head toward the house.

"I was thinking about building a deck and putting in one of those outdoor pizza ovens," he says.

"That would be great! It will be amazing in summer." An image pops into my head of hanging out on the deck, drinking a cold beer and eating pizza, laughing with him.

Shit.

I blink rapidly to remove it.

"You'll probably want to get rid of those pittosporums though," I say. "They're pollinated by blowflies, so you wouldn't want them that close to your deck.

"Wow, you really know your stuff." He gives me an admiring glance.

I scuff my shoes along the grass, feeling my neck heat. Who knew my childhood and teenage years spent as forced labor for my parents would one day come in handy to impress a guy?

"Now, it's my turn to impress you with my lawn-mowing skills," he says.

"I can't wait to see more of your skills," I reply with a wink and he grins at me.

He follows me in his car to my house. I get out the lawn mower and show him how to use it before I start weeding. It's a warm day and halfway through mowing the lawn he strips off his shirt. I try not to ogle too much. I also try desperately not to think about how weeding in the sun while a gorgeous guy mows the lawns and our dogs frolic together is a snapshot of my perfect future.

Preston hated this kind of stuff. On the weekends he wanted to go out to expensive wine bars or restaurants where it was all about being seen with the right people. I'd always felt tense and uptight making conversation with Preston's friends about property prices and expensive overseas holidays, things outside my scope of existence.

The Anonymous Hookup

I watch my anonymous hookup as he tips the last catcher-fill of mown grass into the compost bin.

It seems a bit crazy that the guy is mowing my lawns yet I still don't know his name.

The problem is, in the social media age and especially in a country the size of New Zealand, it's just a hop, skip and a google from sharing names to finding out every detail about his life.

And that feels dangerous. Because at the moment things between us are so easy and straightforward, it's just about laughing, hanging out and hot sex, and I'm worried that might dissolve if real life starts to intrude.

Besides, he said he thought the anonymity thing was hot. Maybe that's part of what's fuelling the incredible sex. I don't want to change the dynamic between us and risk ruining that.

My cock will never forgive me.

He looks up to find me watching him and a grin slides over his face.

"You're looking pretty dirty," he says. "I think it might be time to take a shower."

"Haven't we already showered today?"

"Yes, but not in your shower," he says. "Plus, I don't think there's such a thing as too much shower sex."

"You may have a point," I concede.

Although it turns out this time, fooling around in the shower is only a prelude to the incredible sixty-nine blow jobs we give each other when we stumble out damp and horny.

Afterwards, we lie on my bed in a tangle of limbs and I feel his heart slowing. He skims my back with the lightest of touches and I find myself grazing my fingertips down his arms.

He deposits a lightning-fast kiss to my forehead before pulling away. "Come on, I need sustenance."

"Didn't you just get some?" I grin.

"A man cannot exist on bodily fluids alone." He lightly smacks my ass as he gets up.

We put on some clothes and stumble out to construct a meal from the food in my fridge. We decide on an omelet.

"You want some wine?" My shoulders tense up as I make the offer, because my taste in wine is terrible. Preston tried his hardest to educate me, but apparently I have an unsophisticated palate that will always struggle to deduce different flavors.

"I'm more of a beer guy actually," he says.

I try not to show my relief. "Beer, I can definitely do." I open my fridge. "Is Heineken okay?"

"It's perfect."

So we cook an omelet together and then sit down and eat it, talking about running and gardening and books and TV shows we like.

It's only when we're rinsing the dishes after dinner and he's hassling me about the system I use to load my cutlery—and I'm calling him an uncouth heathen because what kind of feral mingles their knives and forks together?— that I realize we've spent most of the weekend together.

Oops.

We really know how to put the 'extended' into extended anonymous hookup.

But it's okay because we're both in agreement about what this is and isn't.

Chapter Five

Over the next three weeks, Boris and Casper have more play dates than any dogs in history.

I swear they're rolling their eyes at each other in doggie speak for 'yeah, we've got to hang out yet again as our owners are looking for another excuse to hookup.'

Because, okay, it does seem like we're addicted to each other's bodies. We continue to have the hottest sex of my existence. But it's not all sex. We also go running and cook dinner and watch TV together. We even spent an hour one Saturday morning at a garden centre shopping for plants. It's at the garden centre that the anonymous thing trips me up.

I'm inspecting the buxus hedge plants thinking it would be good edging while he's over looking at the herbs.

"Hey," I call out.

He doesn't look up, leaning over to read a label on one of the herb plants.

"Uh... Boris's dad!" I try again.

He still doesn't respond, but the lady next to me gives me a strange look.

"Boris!" I almost shout and this time he looks up.

I beckon to him. He comes over and I show him the buxus and we agree that a hedge would look really good around the outside of the outdoor area he's planning.

As we go to the checkout together, my mind starts to race. It's beyond ridiculous that I still don't know his name.

But if we drop the anonymous thing completely, then what is this? The start of a relationship? Panic floods my chest.

I can't handle the start of a new relationship. My heart is still battered and bruised from my last one.

He carefully places the protective sheet down in the back of his car and I help him transfer his new plants onto it.

"So, I think I need to know your name," I say as we climb into the car. "Because it turns out calling you Boris's dad is a bit embarrassing in public. And I don't want to get into the habit of calling you Boris, because then we'll confuse the hell out of your dog. I really don't want to be moaning in the bedroom and have your dog turn up." I try to keep my voice casual but I'm aware I'm over-explaining, something I often do when I'm nervous.

I look up to find his dark eyes watching me carefully.

"You want to know my name?" he asks slowly.

I can't read the expression on his face.

"First names only?" I suggest. "If you don't want to give me your real name, that's okay. I just need an upgrade on Boris's dad."

He smiles. "Okay."

My shoulders relax.

He gives me a playful look. "You can call me Sam. It may or may not be my real name."

Sam. It suits him. It's a friendly, dependable name.

"Nice to meet you Maybe Sam," I say.

He raises an eyebrow expectantly. "And you are?"

Should I give him a false name? Somehow, I really, really don't want to do that.

"You can call me Lane," I say.

"Lane, as in a beautiful country lane we could go for a Sunday drive down?"

"Yep, you got me. My real name is actually cul-de-sac, but I figure Lane is a good alternative."

He smiles as he starts the engine.

And then we drive back to his house and spend the rest of the afternoon working together in his backyard while Boris and Casper happily chew on the plastic containers the plants came in.

So now I know his first name might or might not be Sam.

And as we continue to hang out, the list grows of other things I know about him.

Because you can't hang out with someone the amount of time we've been spending together without picking up on stuff.

I know he's really smart, but he's more of a word shark than a mathematician, because when we watch *Eight out of Ten Cats does Countdown* one Friday night, he gets all the word puzzles immediately, but has this adorable frown when he's trying to solve the math problems.

Whatever he does for a job, he's good at it. He has to work late a few times, and often has to respond to emails and phone calls in a way that makes me conclude he's not a pleb at the bottom of the ladder. But his work outfits have puzzled me, because sometimes he wears a suit and other times he's more casually dressed in slacks and a tidy sweater.

Tonight he messages me to say he has to work late but asks if I'm okay with him coming over afterwards, and even though we've spent every night together so far this week, I almost sprain a finger replying to him so quickly to tell him to come over whenever he wants.

I use the chance to catch up on some of my lesson planning and marking until my heart leaps when there's a knock on my door.

I stash my marking in a box and shove it in the study before padding down the hallway to answer the door, Casper at my heels.

Maybe Sam's dressed in a suit tonight, Boris at his side.

His stubble rasps against my skin as he leans forward to brush a kiss on my cheek. I turn, nudging his nose so I can capture his lips in a proper kiss. We kiss softly, sweetly. Then he rests his forehead on mine for a few seconds before he draws back.

"You look tired," I say.

"I had a full-on day," he says.

"Have you eaten?" I ask as we walk down the hallway, the dogs charging ahead. "I saved some dinner for you."

His eyes soften. "Thanks, but I grabbed a bite at work."

"Bedtime then?"

"Oh, I'm always in the mood for bed," he says with a grin.

We get the dogs settled and then head to the bathroom together. And okay, your anonymous hookup having his own toothbrush in your bathroom might seem strange to some people, but we spend most nights together at the moment, so it's practical that we have toothbrushes at each other's houses. I ignore the warm feeling I get from doing this small domestic routine together.

He catches my gaze in the mirror and arches one of his gorgeous eyebrows before he spits out the foam.

"Are you admiring the sexy way I brush my teeth?" he asks.

"Is it actually possible for someone to brush their teeth sexily?"

He grins. "I think I'm up to the challenge."

Of course, he does exaggerated tooth brushing, sucking seductively on the end of his toothbrush, which looks so ridiculous and makes me laugh so hard I'm breathless before we even start kissing.

We stumble back, my knees hitting the edge of the bed before falling backwards. His body is a delicious weight on top of me, his lips finding mine like they're superpowered magnets.

Before this can heat up any further, his phone chimes.

I wrench my lips away from his. "You want to get that?"

"Definitely not," he says as he nuzzles into my neck.

But it's no sooner stopped ringing than it starts again.

"Damn."

He reluctantly pulls away from me and picks his phone up from the bedside table. He frowns at it.

"Sorry, I need to take this."

He disappears out of the bedroom.

My mind speculates on what his call is about.

Is he a doctor and the hospital needs his opinion on something? But I've seen no trace of him being on call, so I'm pretty sure anything medical is out. Is he a lawyer? An accountant? To afford his house he has to be on a fairly decent pay packet, but somehow the more I get to know him, the less corporate he seems.

The anonymity thing, which was my idea, now feels more and more ludicrous.

He comes back into the bedroom wearing a frown.

"Everything okay?" I ask.

"Yeah, it was my mother."

"Is she okay?" I ask.

"She's fine."

Despite his words, he's twitchy as he lies down, almost vibrating with something pent up.

I can tell he wants to talk, and I'm surprised to find how eager I am to hear what he has to say.

I've been collecting all these little observations about him and about what makes him tick, so the idea of getting more information directly is appealing.

I roll onto my side to face him. "So, what's your mum like?" I ask.

"Amazing." The word is out of his mouth immediately. He scrapes a hand along the stubble on his jaw. "She's incredibly vibrant with a larger-than-life personality."

"Are you close?"

"Yeah we are. We have lots of fun together and we definitely share the same sense of humor."

"Is that who I should blame it on?" I tease.

He smiles, but then his smile fades.

"I'm sensing there's a but coming," I say.

"There should always be a butt somewhere," he reaches over and strokes his hand lightly up my ass.

I roll my eyes as I batt his hand away. "But..." I prompt.

He heaves a deep sigh. "But she can be a handful sometimes. She had me when she was seventeen, so it feels like we grew up together."

"Do you know your dad?" I ask quietly.

He shakes his head. "She conceived me from a one-night stand at a random party she'd crashed. She didn't even know his first name."

I laugh. "Imagine not knowing your hook-up's name."

He grins. "Yeah, imagine that. At least we were never in danger of you getting me pregnant"

"I think we can pretty much guarantee that."

His grin fades and his face grows serious. "I was her entire life for so long, and I'm grateful for everything she sacrificed for me. I understand how hard it is for her to let go, but I'm trying to put up some boundaries, you know? I'm fairly sure an overbearing mother is not top of the list of what every man is looking for in a partner and I swear she'd still be inquiring if I'm changing my underwear regularly if she could."

"I'll be happy to report that your underwear changing habits are sufficient," I say.

He laughs his deep chuckle. "Thanks."

"And I can see why it's hard, trying to draw back from someone you love," I say.

His eyes soften and he shuffles closer to me, putting his hand on my hip, his fingers warm on my skin.

He studies me. "What's your family like?"

My chest tightens.

"I've got three brothers and two sisters, so my upbringing was the opposite of yours," I say. "There was never enough attention to go around."

"What number are you?"

"I'm number five. Not quite the baby."

He's looking at me with such... interest, the words spill out of me.

"By the time I came along, it was like my parents had been there, done that. Almost as if they were bored with parenting and nothing I did would ever be interesting enough to capture their interest."

Fuck. I've never said that out loud before. It's something buried deep in my psyche, that feeling of inadequacy that I could never do anything different from my siblings, never stand out from the crowd.

He places a kiss on the side of my head.

"I can't imagine you failing to capture someone's interest," he whispers.

My mind whirls.

Was that why I'd been so flattered by Preston initially? I was finishing up my teacher training when we met and I'd been so amazed I'd attracted the interest of an older, more successful guy. Me, Lane, always the overlooked one, even among the people who were supposed to love me.

But it turned out Preston's interest was conditional. He wasn't interested in the real me, only in the version of me he wanted to turn me into.

"You'd be surprised." My voice is flat.

"Maybe somewhere in between our experiences is the right balance," he suggests.

"Definitely."

His dark eyes scan my face and I stare straight back.

"Thanks for letting me vent," he says.

"Anytime." I try to communicate with my eyes how much I mean that.

Okay, I might still not know his full name, but I'm starting to know *him*. I know he's a good person who cares about people. I can imagine it's difficult trying not to upset someone he loves while still carving out space to be independent.

He reaches over and trails a fingertip down my cheek in a gesture so intimate my breath rushes out of me.

He leans forward to place a gentle kiss on my lips. This kiss feels different from our usual ones. It starts off gentle, sweet. As if it's the kiss version of a thank you. *Thank you for being here. Thank you for listening.*

It deepens yet stays tender. I move so I'm on top of him, continuing to kiss him deeply. Our cocks decide to get into the action, and I feel him hardening against me.

I try to reinforce my words with my body, stroking down his warm skin, trying to let him know that it's acceptable to not be able to please other people all the time, that he's perfect the way he is.

I work him open incredibly slowly and patiently, one finger then two, enjoying every gasp and shudder from him until his head lolls, eyes glassy.

And I'm fairly sure everything he does, from the way he locks his legs around me after I slide inside him, to how he cups his hand to my cheek, his gaze not leaving mine...I'm certain he's trying to communicate something to me too.

***

The next evening we're hanging out at his place doing the Netflix component of our 'Netflix and Chill'. Is it weird that I like the Netflix part of it almost as much as I like the Chill? Just the two of us together on the couch. Initially we kept to separate parts of the couch, but somehow that's changed over the past three weeks and now at least one part of his body is always in contact with me.

Tonight, he's got his arm casually draped around me as we watch *Brooklyn Nine-Nine* while I hassle him about his obvious crush on Andy Samberg, the actor who plays Jake Peralta.

"I just admire him for his ability to deliver those one-line zingers," he says.

"Sure, it's just about his zingers," I say, and he chuckles.

His phone chimes, and he picks it up, making a face.

"Is it your mum again?" I ask.

"No, just work. I'll be right back."

He stands up. I hear him answer the phone in his deep voice, then the sound fades as he closes the door to the hallway.

I stare at the frozen faces on the screen, my mind churning.

Is it time to suggest moving past the anonymity thing? It was fun to start with, a reminder this isn't a proper relationship, but I have an irrational craving to know about his life now. I want him to be able to vent to me about problems he's having at work, like he talked to me about his mother.

It seems ridiculous that I know so many other things about him now, yet I'm ignorant of the fundamentals of his full name and what he does.

To distract myself from overthinking, I log on to the chess app to find I've received a series of messages from Charles Dickens over the past day.

Charles Dickens: *It's your move.*

Then, three hours later...

Charles Dickens: *YOUR MOVE!!!*

Two hours later...

Charles Dickens: *I've done some calculations and have determined that your response time has increased from 2 hours to 13 hours over the past three weeks. Don't tell me this means you went out and found yourself a life??*

I fire a quick message back. *Maybe it just means that my brain is slowing down.*

Charles Dickens isn't online right now, but I make my

move anyway. All going well, I might capture his rook out of that capital piece exchange.

I quickly type another message to Charles Dickens. *Beat that buttercup.*

The door to the hallway opens and Maybe Sam reappears.

"Sorry about that," he says.

I quickly shut down the app and stash my phone in my pocket.

He follows the movement, one eyebrow quirking.

"Are you sexting someone?" He's trying for a jovial tone, but it fails to launch.

My heart thumps. I don't want to admit I'm playing online chess. Preston always gave me crap about it being an old man's hobby.

Instead, I just go for another simple truth. "I haven't looked in another guy's direction since we started hooking up."

His face relaxes. "Me neither."

We stare at each other for a few heartbeats. Then he smiles and I smile back.

When he sits down next to me, we join those smiles together in a sweet kiss.

I settle against him, his arm automatically coming around me as he uses the remote to restart the program.

What we don't talk about is how that isn't supposed to be in the guidelines of hooking up.

Chapter Six

The following day my head spins. What does it mean we admitted we're exclusive? That we've spent nearly every night together for the past three weeks?

Luckily, I have ten nervous teenagers to distract me from my mulling.

"Those kids from the flash private schools are going to look down on us," Rosa says. She's sitting in the front seat of the school van next to me, wearing a scowl on her face as if she's already been insulted. Some of my students from difficult backgrounds have an understandable chip on their shoulder, approaching the world anticipating the things that are going to go wrong.

"Do you know what one of my favorite sayings is?" I ask as I turn onto the ramp that will take me onto the motorway.

"No, but I'm guessing you're about to tell me," she snarks, and I try to hide my smile. Rosa's tough outer shell hides a warm gooey center.

"It's from Eleanor Roosevelt. Do you know who that is?"

Rosa shakes her head.

"She was married to the president of the United States, but she was an incredible woman in her own right. Google her sometime. Anyway, one quote from her is 'No one can make you feel inferior without your consent'."

She slumps against the door, picking at her fingernail. "What does that mean, Sir?"

"It means the decision on whether you feel like other people are better than you is entirely yours, not theirs. People might look down on you, but you get to be the one who decides whether it makes you feel inadequate. It's the idea that you can't control the behavior of other people. You can only control your response to it."

"That kind of makes sense," she says grudgingly.

"It's an important thing to remember, because there will always be people who try to make you feel bad about yourself," I say. "But you're the one who decides if you let them."

Rosa just raises an eyebrow in response. I don't know if I got through to her or not. Sometimes with teenagers you think they've absorbed nothing, only to have them surprise you months later with a comment that shows they were actually listening.

I pull into the carpark outside Pinnacle studios and my chattering students instantly go quiet as they take in the modern building with its sleek lines and perfectly landscaped gardens.

Yep, we're not at Southlake High School anymore, Toto.

I lead ten wide-eyed students into a reception area, decked out in cobalt blue and white tones, and providing as much warmth as an iceberg.

The receptionist behind the front desk seems in tune with the icy theme. She raises a snooty eyebrow. "Can I help you?"

"These are the students from Southlake High."

Her face loses some of its rigidity and she nods. "'I'll call Claire. She'll be here shortly.

"Thanks." I step back to my students, who are surveying the reception area as if they've just landed on Mars.

Luckily 'shortly' is accurate, and it's barely a minute before an attractive brunette bustles out into the reception area. She breaks into a huge smile when she sees us.

"Lane!" She gives my hand an enthusiastic shake. "Hi, I'm Claire."

"It's so nice to finally meet you."

She smiles at me. "I feel I know you already after your emails."

"Ditto."

She extends her welcoming smile to my students. "Follow me, guys."

As she leads us down a corridor, she lowers her voice. "I've paired you with my favorite director, who's also a close friend of mine. Have any of you seen *Getting the Goons*?"

"Yeah, it's sick," Tabitha says.

"I love that show," Elroy says.

I grin. *Getting the Goons* is a local comedy drama with a cult following due to its snappy dialogue and offbeat characters. Yeah, my students are going to have ultimate swagger rights when they get back to school.

We arrive at an editing studio, where a man sitting at a desk peers at the footage on a computer screen.

Claire strides up and taps him on the shoulder. "The students from Southlake are here."

He turns around in his chair, a wide smile on his face.

My breath leaves me.

No. It can't be.

Because I know that smile. I saw it when I left his bed this morning.

"This is Sam Heaney everyone," Claire says as he stands up.

"Hi guys," Sam says to my students.

"And this is their teacher, Lane Fenwick," Claire says.

His gaze flicks to me and his smile dies an instant death. Shock overtakes his face.

We just stare at each other.

I'm suddenly aware Claire and ten students are watching us, curiosity emitting from each of them as the seconds tick by.

I pull on every ounce of my teacher's professionalism and plaster on a polite smile.

"Uh... nice to meet you, Sam." I extend my hand.

He blinks rapidly. "You too, Lane."

It's weird shaking his warm hand, a hand I know so well, a hand that has touched me a thousand times over the past month. Yeah, things not to think about right now.

He gives my hand a small squeeze before letting go.

Then he blows out a breath before he turns to my students.

"Right, are you ready to learn how to make your own TV show?"

* * *

Watching my anonymous hookup, also known as Sam Heaney, TV director, interacting with my students is the definition of surreal.

Talk about two worlds colliding. This is two worlds smashing into each other with a force that could crack open the galaxy.

Sam talks them through the process of storyboarding and camera shots, then sets them loose with video cameras to have a go themselves.

"Sir, sir, you need to come see this!" Rosa calls out to me from the other side of the room.

She's got footage of Tobias doing the most dramatic dying sequence I've ever seen, hand over heart, gurgling loudly as he falls to the ground.

Tobias is one of my most reserved students, a guy who has intense allergies and hides behind his thick glasses and long fringe. I love seeing him coming out of his shell and performing for the camera.

"That's some quality gurgling," I tell Tobias, who gives a shy grin.

When I glance up, Sam's watching me with a smile.

By the time lunchtime rolls around, my students chat excitedly as we head to the reception area where a buffet of food has been set up for them.

When we arrive, the students from the two other schools are also there.

And yes, they're kids from private schools, but they appear as overawed by their surroundings as my students, and as they chat, talking about what directors they are working with and what they've been doing, the differences between them seem to diminish.

Sam sidles up to me. "So... Lane Fenwick," he says.

"So... Sam Heaney," I reply.

We grin at each other and, holy hell, for a moment I want to kiss him. Until now, I've been able to kiss him whenever the mood strikes me, so it seems a special type of torture to have his lips this close and not be able to claim them with mine.

"Is this as insane for you as it is for me?" he asks in a low voice.

"Watching you teach my students? Yep, that's definitely in the insane basket."

"I thought you might be a teacher," he says.

"Really? Do I use my teacher's voice with you?"

He chuckles. "Something about you gives out instructional vibes."

The fact he's been speculating about what I do shouldn't surprise me because I've devoted time to trying to work out what he does, but somehow it does.

"I'd never have guessed you're a director," I say.

Claire comes over to us. "How's the morning gone?" she asks me.

"Great. The students are really enjoying it."

"I'm so glad."

"They're a smart group of kids," Sam says.

"So, Lane, how long have you been a teacher for?" Claire flutters her eyelashes at me.

Oh shit. I throw a 'help me' look at Sam.

"Um... Claire," Sam says.

"Yeah?"

"He bats for my team."

Claire's face falls as she looks between us. "Are you sure?"

I huff out a half-laugh.

Sam scratches at his jaw. "Yeah, you could say I've had some conclusive proof."

Claire's smile rebounds as quickly as it had faded. "I knew it! I knew there was a weird vibe between you two when I introduced you."

Sam scoffs. "I don't do weird vibes."

Claire studies me for a second, then turns back to Sam. "Wait, this isn't the guy you were telling me about, is it?"

My pulse skitters as Sam sends me an apologetic look. "Um...yeah."

"Wait, what level of telling are you talking about? Because if details of any parts of my anatomy have been shared, then I'm going to go hide in the storeroom for the rest of the day. Or potentially wait in the carpark," I say.

Claire rolls her eyes. "Sam doesn't kiss and tell. He's just been extremely happy for the past few weeks, and under forced interrogation admitted it was because of a guy."

My gaze darts to him. Is there a blush trekking up Sam's cheeks?

Sam's been so happy his friend picked up on it? A flush of warmth goes through me at that idea.

"Sir, do you think this sandwich has mayonnaise in it?" Tobias comes across to me and I snap my attention back to my job.

* * *

The afternoon is just as surreal. My students finish learning how to operate the cameras and then start storyboarding the project they're going to be working on next time.

We're in a rush to leave so I can get the students back to school in time for buses home, so I don't have time for anything more than a quick goodbye to Sam.

"OMG, that was so cool," Viliami says as soon as we're inside the van.

"We got the best director to work with," Tobias says.

"I can't believe he directs *Getting the Goons*. Izzie's going to be so jealy when I tell her," Tabitha says.

The Anonymous Hookup

"I thought directors are supposed to be old, but he's young and hot," Rosa says.

My stomach hollows.

That's right. It turns out my anonymous hookup is a hotshot TV director, and now he knows I'm only a teacher.

Now the anonymity thing has been blown, is he still going to be interested in things continuing? Maybe that was a big part of the attraction for him. The fact I could be anyone, a blank slate to project whatever fantasy he wanted onto.

Yep, it appears my insecurities are well and truly winning the battle in my head right now.

I get back to school and am checking the notes from my substitute teacher about how my other classes behaved when my phone beeps with a message.

My place or yours?

So it looks like he wants it to continue. At least for tonight.

Mine.

My rationale is purely practical. It's a cold night, and my house has a good wood burner. I'm not going to focus on how much I like the idea of Sam and me together in front of a cozy fire.

Do you want me to grab Casper from doggie daycare when I pick up Boris?

That would be great, thanks. I'll let Erin know.

Great. I don't want to be accused of dognapping.

Yeah, I wouldn't want you to get a criminal record.

When Sam, Boris and Casper turn up on my doorstep promptly at six, Casper greets me with his usual enthusiastic tail wag.

"Thanks for picking him up," I say.

"You should have seen the look Erin gave me," he comments as the dogs bound down the hallway ahead of us.

"Did she say anything?"

"She asked me if we'd managed to have any play dates."

"What did you say to that?"

"I said we'd managed one or two."

As we reach the kitchen, I chuckle and head to the fridge while Sam pulls up on the other side of the breakfast bar.

"So Lane, anything interesting happen to you at work today?" he asks with a wide grin.

I hand him a beer. "Nah Sam, it was just a standard, average day."

He tips his head back and laughs.

Some of the tension inside me eases, because okay, he might be a hotshot TV director, but he's also the guy who laughs at my jokes, who loves his dog, who doesn't know anything about gardening. He's the guy who can cook a mean carbonara and omelet, who prefers beer to wine, the guy who has a complicated relationship with his mother.

After we've played with the dogs and eaten, we don't switch on the TV like normal. Instead we curl up on the couch facing each other and talk, Boris and Casper happily snoozing together on the other couch.

Sam tells me about his work and how he originally wanted to be a theatre director, but took a film paper at university and decided that television was the right medium of storytelling for him and he's never looked back.

I talk to him about teaching and my students and school and the feeling you get when you can see you're getting through to a student, that you're making a difference in their life.

We talk and talk and talk until I suddenly realize it's

after 2am. Then we stumble off to bed and I drift off to sleep with Sam holding me close.

I blearily wake up the next morning early, because my body has always refused to sleep in properly even when I've had a late night.

Despite my lack of sleep, my mind starts ticking and doesn't stop, especially when I realize something major.

Sam and I didn't have sex last night. We were too busy talking.

The anonymity thing has been blown off its hinges. I think Sam now knows more about me than anyone except Jules.

Sam stirs and when I look at him, his dark eyes blink sleepily at me. How is it that Sam like this — sleepy eyed, hair tousled, pillow crease on his face — is more gorgeous to me than he's been at any other time?

Something inside me clenches.

We've failed on the anonymous part, and last night we failed on the hookup part, so what the hell is our definition now?

I feel the itch to address it, to get us back on a firm footing.

"You look like you're thinking too hard for this time in the morning," he says, his voice scratchy with sleep.

"I'm just thinking we need another definition change, because we're not exactly anonymous anymore," I say.

Sam stretches, giving me a view of his gorgeous chest. "No, Lane Fenwick, we can definitely no longer classify this as anonymous."

"A no-strings affair?" I offer as I sit up, the duvet sliding off me.

An emotion flashes across his face, but it's gone before I can name it.

"You're the English teacher. Coming up with words is your thing," he says.

"Yeah, because your job requires you to be mute, TV director."

He laughs and sits up too, leaning over to nuzzle his nose between my neck and shoulder.

I turn to kiss him, and we forget about definitions for a while.

Chapter Seven

Two days later, I open the front door to Sam and Boris with an enormous smile on my face. He lets Boris off the lead and the dog bounds down the hall to find Casper.

"You've been keeping secrets," Sam says, shaking his head at me.

My chest constricts. Sam knows almost everything there is to know about me now. What does he think I've kept from him? The only thing I haven't told him is about my online chess addiction, which I'd like to think doesn't count as something major.

"What secrets?" I croak out.

His dark eyes dance. "Social media stalking informed me today is a special day."

Oh god. That.

"Ah...yeah."

"Happy birthday." He pulls a gift bag from behind his back, brandishing it with a flourish.

I freeze. I stare at the present like it's a grenade about to explode.

"Thanks." I take the present off him and step back to let him in.

"It's not much," Sam says as we reach the living room.

I sit down on the couch, still holding the gift bag gingerly. "You didn't need to get me anything."

Sam plops down on the couch next to me. "Are you going to open it?"

"Sure." I try to pump some enthusiasm into my voice.

Okay, it's weird to freak out about receiving a present, but my track record isn't great.

Preston and I were together for three years. In the first year, he'd gotten me a wine-tasting course so I could learn to share his love of wine. I'd hated his disappointment when, at the end of the weekend, I'd still been unable to tell the difference between fruity and floral flavors.

The second year we were together he'd gotten me an expensive cashmere sweater, somehow convinced that cashmere would be the exception to my wool allergy. The ugly rash I broke out in the first time I wore the sweater was strong evidence to the contrary.

Last year, he'd gotten me a voucher for an expensive resort in Taupō so we could have a romantic weekend together. It had stressed me out because I knew he'd want to do lots of expensive things while we were there and I couldn't expect him to pay for the whole weekend.

Sure enough, I'd spent most of our trip trying not to calculate the growing hole in my savings.

I take a deep breath and open Sam's gift bag.

Inside is a blue T-shirt. I unfold it to discover a quote written across the front.

So we beat on, boats against the current, borne ceaselessly back into the past.

The Anonymous Hookup

My heart pounds. It's my favorite quote from *The Great Gatsby*.

I hold the soft cotton in my hands, trying to collect myself.

Sam knows me. He really knows me.

"I love this quote," I whisper.

When I raise my gaze, the smile Sam gives me is pure happiness. "I thought you might."

"How on earth did you have time to find this T-shirt if you only just found out it was my birthday today?"

After all, it wasn't exactly a common item you could buy at the nearest store.

He scratches his nose, color rising up his neck. "I may have found someone online who prints quotes on T-shirts and may have called him up and arranged to drive out to Albany to pick one up from him."

My eyebrows shoot up.

It's an hour's drive from his work to Albany. Each way.

I can't believe he did that for me.

Suddenly I have to kiss him so badly I'll combust if I don't.

Sam kisses me back with the same level of enthusiasm, his tongue finding mine as we sink back into the couch, continuing to kiss.

Things are just heating up when there's a knock on the door.

Sam wrenches his mouth away from mine. "Are you expecting someone?"

"No."

I stand up, and as I walk down the hallway toward the front door, I try to calm down parts of my body into the appropriate-to-be-answering-the-door mode.

I open it to find Jules standing there.

She holds up a bottle of wine with a smile. "Hey, best friend, I brought you birthday drinks. I know you hate all things to do with today, but I didn't want you to be alone."

I scrape my foot along the floor. "Um... I'm actually not alone. Sam's here."

"Sam, your anonymous hookup, who's not quite so anonymous anymore?" She grins. And okay, I might have messaged her a few OMG's from the TV studio.

"We're now classifying our relationship as a no-strings affair, actually."

"A no strings affair. Right." She stretches out that last word like it's a piece of chewing gum, giving me a smirk.

"So, are you coming in?" I ask, because I can't leave my best friend on my doorstep when she's come to surprise me on my birthday, no matter how much she potentially deserves it right now.

Sam looks up as we come into the room, and I get an off-kilter feeling for a second, like two more worlds are colliding.

"Sam, this is Jules. Jules, Sam."

Sam's face splits into a grin. "Ah, Jules, the best friend."

"Sam the... actually, I've lost track of what your official definition is now," Jules says. I scowl at her.

"Jules just popped in. She's not staying long," I blurt.

"But it looks like she brought you some wine," Sam says. "It'd be rude to take the wine and turf her out before you open the bottle."

"Wine really is the best gift in that way," Jules says happily as she heads into my kitchen.

"Because you'll end up consuming more of my present than I do?" I suggest.

"Exactly." She's already getting wineglasses out of the cupboard. I follow her into the kitchen.

"You want some wine or beer?" I ask Sam.

"If I stick to my heathenistic ways and say beer, will you judge me?" he asks.

"Oh totally, but I've already judged you for lots of things, so what's one more?" I grab a bottle of beer out of the fridge and open it for him.

I head over to the couch to hand it to him and he grins at me, doing this nose-scrunching thing. I can't help doing it back.

"Are you having some of your birthday wine?" Jules asks me.

"Sure, as long as you don't expect me to provide an in-depth analysis of the flavor."

Jules rolls her eyes. "Yeah, that's not exactly my top priority when I'm drinking wine." She unscrews the bottle and pours two glasses, brings them across and hands me one.

"Thanks."

I take my seat next to Sam and she settles into an armchair opposite the couch. My heart thuds. Something about this set up reminds me of an interrogation.

"So, you've managed to survive the day then," Jules says.

"Just," I say.

"Why would you be worried about him surviving the day?" Sam asks.

"Lane's not a fan of birthdays," Jules explains.

"How do you not like birthdays?" Sam says. "It's like not liking kittens or rainbows."

"I'm sure people who have allergies to cats don't particularly like kittens," I point out.

"It's like not liking pictures of kittens then," he counters, and I laugh.

Jules looks between us, her forehead creasing.

Sam's phone chimes.

"It's Evan. I've got to take this," he says apologetically.

Evan is his assistant director, a fact that I now know. I give him an understanding nod as he walks away.

Jules waits until he's out of the room before turning to me, her eyes wide.

"Wow," she says.

I'm not surprised that Sam has inspired that reaction from her.

"He's something else, isn't he?" I say, cursing the fact I can't hide the wistfulness in my voice.

"Well, he seems like a great guy, but that wasn't what I meant," she says.

My forehead creases. "What did you mean then?"

"I've never seen you like this before with someone."

"Like what?"

"You're so... you... around him." She waves a hand in the air as if that explains everything.

"What do you mean by that?"

"With Preston you were so buttoned up, trying to be the perfect boyfriend. You were like that with your boyfriends at uni too, but with Sam, you're yourself. No pretenses."

"Well, we started as an anonymous hookup," I point out.

"It's definitely not hookup territory anymore, is it? He looks at you like I look at a packet of walnut brittle."

"I take it that's a good thing?"

"It's a very good thing."

I try to hide the happy flush that races through me at her words, but Jules gives me a knowing look, indicating I haven't hidden anything particularly well.

Luckily Sam comes back into the room before she has a chance to delve further.

"We were just talking about you," she says cheerfully to Sam.

"Oh good. I do like to be the topic of conversation. What aspect of me were you discussing? My rugged good looks or my charming personality? I know, it's so hard to decide which one to focus on when there's fertile ground to cover for both of them," Sam says as he settles back on the couch next to me.

"It was actually your humble nature we dwelt on," I say.

He deposits a quick kiss to my temple. "Another worthy topic of conversation," he agrees.

"Everything about you is worthy," I say in a voice filled with innuendo, the sole purpose of which is to make Jules choke on her drink.

It works.

"So, Sam, tell me all about yourself..." Jules says when she's recovered from her spluttering.

"What do you want to know?" he asks.

"Do you want to have kids someday?" she asks with an evil grin.

Now it's my turn to choke on the wine.

"Yeah, I've always wanted kids," Sam says easily.

I try to ignore how my heart soars at his words, because that was another point of contention between Preston and me. He didn't want his lifestyle to ever change with the inconvenience of kids, while I couldn't imagine my life not including a family someday.

But I shouldn't care if my no-strings affair partner's thoughts about kids align with mine, right? Right???

Jules and Sam continue to chat like they've known each

other forever, occasionally hassling me and each other, while a warm feeling spreads through me.

I'm not sure if it's the glass of wine I'm drinking that's giving me this happy glow.

* * *

After Jules finally leaves, Sam turns to me. "So, birthday boy, I'm thinking that because you've reached the ancient age of twenty-six, you might need your rest."

"Why do I suspect this is just a ploy to get me to bed?"

He winks at me. "Am I that transparent?"

I laugh and he grins too, tugging me towards my room.

I love how familiar and comfortable this feels. Sam and I getting ready for bed together, stripping down to our boxers, climbing into bed.

To my surprise, Sam doesn't reach for me immediately. Instead, he props himself up on an elbow to look at me. "So, do you want to tell me why you don't like birthdays?" he asks.

I shrug. "I don't know."

But Sam doesn't let me get away with that. He reaches out and runs his hand up and down my arm, waiting patiently.

I don't want to tell him about my experiences with Preston, so I go to my original reason for not liking birthdays.

"I guess my parents didn't make a big deal out of birthdays, so the best way to stop being disappointed was not to expect anything."

I feel stupid as I say the words. It's such a dumb thing to get upset about.

Our family photo albums were full of photos of large

parties for my eldest siblings' milestone birthdays, parties that had stopped by the time I came along.

"One year they forgot about my birthday completely," I say quietly.

Sam's breath hitches. "Really?"

"It was when I turned fourteen. Actually, it's not true they forgot completely. My mother remembered after dinner."

Sam's silent for a moment, watching me with his dark eyes.

"My mother used to make me watch the video of my birth on my birthday," he says finally.

I choke out a laugh. "You've got to be kidding."

"Oh, how I wish I were. She claims it was the most beautiful moment of her life. All I saw was a seventeen-year-old screaming the ward down while the most disgusting thing in the world slithered out of her." He shudders.

"The most disgusting thing in the world was you, right?"

"Yeah. I improved as I got older."

I smile. "You definitely did."

Sam strokes my side, his fingers leaving a trail of shivers.

"Maybe I can change your mind about birthdays," he suggests.

"How are you planning to do that?"

He answers me by leaning forward and putting his lips on mine.

And okay, I'm totally on board with this method of persuasion.

We sink into the kiss. Sam's kiss is gentle yet intense which should be a contradiction but somehow isn't.

He eventually prises his lips off mine, leaving me

breathless, as he slides down my body, kissing a line down my chest. He pauses over one of my nipples then pulls one into his mouth. I give a low moan and he throws me a lopsided smile before he continues kissing down my stomach.

Lower.

Lower.

He lingers around my abs while I try not to levitate off the bed with want.

When he finally takes pity on me and takes me into the warm heat of his mouth, I almost combust.

"Sam." God, my voice sounds so strung out it's barely recognizable.

He pulls his mouth off my cock with a wet pop.

"I like it when you say my name," he says. His smile has a shy edge to it I've never seen before.

Our eyes meet and the warmth in his gaze causes my heart to race faster.

I don't have a chance to respond before he's ducked his head again, depositing a gentle kiss on the head of my cock before taking it into his mouth again.

But his lips remain gentle, and he sucks only lightly, starting a slow torturous friction that has me trembling.

He shuts his eyes, his eyelashes fluttering against his cheeks; those long eyelashes that I once used as evidence to convince myself that he was a decent person. How is that only a month ago?

I close my own eyes, losing myself in the bliss of feeling. Sam seems determined to string this out, to prolong my pleasure as he moves soft lips over me.

Suddenly I feel his fingers grazing the sensitive skin behind my balls, and then further back as he circles my hole with slow, teasing brushes.

My breath hitches as his finger finally, finally slips inside.

"Oh God," I cry out.

"No, remember, my name is Sam," he says.

I huff out a laugh, but it stops when I meet his gaze. I don't think anyone has ever stared at me like this before. As if he really, really likes what he sees.

For a few heartbeats we remain locked in each other's gazes.

And then he's slithering up my body, kissing me so forcefully it steals my breath away.

"Sorry, I just had to do that."

"It's okay," I gasp.

And he's back down my body to continue his mission of turning me into a squirming, quivering mess.

He's so focused on me, on every little gasp and sigh I make,

My breathing shudders.

This is not hook-up sex.

This is sex where he knows my body well, when I have complete and utter trust in him, where there's something else swirling between us besides lust and desire.

"Please," I beg when I can't stand it anymore, my voice coming out thin and needy.

And suddenly he snaps a condom on and he's hovering over me, his breath warm on my face.

"Lane," he says the word like a caress.

A shiver goes down my spine at the sound of my name falling from his lips.

Then he's sliding inside me, filling me up.

Oh god.

Sam groans as he moves further in and I feel it vibrate through my body.

I arch my ass up because nothing matters more than having more of Sam inside me.

He bottoms out, his face buried in my neck, his breath rough in my ear.

He stays there for a second, placing a gentle kiss on my neck.

Then he pulls back and starts to move, rocking gently at first, then more intensely when he gets the angle right, lighting me up from the inside.

The entire time his gaze doesn't leave my face.

Somehow it feels like the bravest thing I've ever done, to meet Sam's gaze squarely right now.

Because this isn't about simply chasing an orgasm. This is something else entirely.

But I don't want to deprive myself of seeing him like this; his face flushed, his pupils dilated, hair messy from where my hands were running through it earlier.

He leans forward to kiss me and our lips and tongues meet messily yet perfectly, as if our kiss is a metaphor for this thing between us. Messy and perfect.

"I'm going to..." He groans and then I feel him pulsing inside me.

It only takes a few tugs of my own cock before I'm there too, my mind going offline as pleasure rips through my body. Holy hell. My thighs cramp with the intensity of it.

"Happy birthday," he murmurs to me.

It's probably the first time I've ever felt like this. Adored. Treasured.

I'm trembling and it's not just the come-down of the most intense orgasm of my life.

Because this is so far past a hookup now. And if I'm being honest with myself, it's way past a no-strings affair. I don't want to start cataloging how far past that we are. I try to switch off my brain because I don't want to start cataloging the swirl of emotions I have for Sam.

I have a feeling I'll freak out if I try.

Falling for him wasn't supposed to be part of this.

I stir the next morning as Sam gently pulls away from me. Apparently we spent the night wrapped around each other yet again.

"Sorry, early start," he says.

"It's okay." My voice sounds croaky.

I stretch and blink a few times to remind my eyes how they're supposed to work before they manage to focus on Sam buttoning up his shirt.

"I'm busy tonight," he says apologetically. "It's a work thing."

"That's alright."

Maybe it's for the best. A night apart to give my head a chance to stop swirling. To work out exactly what this is.

He comes back to the bed to kiss me. We linger over the kiss, because kissing Sam isn't something that should ever be hurried. His warm lips, his taste, the rough scrape of his stubble... I don't think I'll ever get enough of kissing Sam.

"Have a great day," he says after he pulls away.

"I'll try."

Chapter Eight

Sam told me to have a great day. I'm not sure if his definition of 'great' includes me spending the entire day obsessing over what the hell we're doing.

Last night... was incredible. Actually, it was beyond incredible. It was the most intense sex I've ever had. I've never felt so connected to a person, ever.

And it scares me because we've moved so far from what this started as, it's almost unrecognizable.

Even teaching my classes can't completely distract me from my churning mind.

After my last class I head back to my office to do some of the endless marking that is the bane of every English teacher's existence, but I find it difficult to focus. My mind keeps slipping back to Sam.

Maybe chess is a good way to get my mind off things? I log into the app on my phone and see the light next to Charles Dickens's name that shows he's online. Good. Charles Dickens and I are currently embroiled in an epic match. We've just done a queen exchange, so it's now going

The Anonymous Hookup

to be a slog to the end as we try to out-manoeuvre each other with our remaining capital pieces.

I make my next move, shifting my knight to threaten his bishop. Charles Dickens counters almost immediately by sliding his bishop on the diagonal to the other end of the board. I narrow my eyes suspiciously, as it's now hovering slightly too close to my king for comfort.

A bubble floats which indicates Charles Dickens is sending me a message.

Charles Dickens: *What does one pirate say when they beat the other in chess?*

ChessLover365: *Are you trying to distract me?*

Charles Dickens: *Damn, I should have known you'd see through my master plan.*

I try to turn my attention back to the board, but I can't stop myself from wondering what the hell chess playing pirates say.

ChessLover365: *Shit, it's working. Okay, you better tell me what the pirate says.*

Charles Dickens: *Check matey!*

I laugh out loud as I return my attention to his bishop. If I move my rook next to it, he'll have to move his bishop, which will give me a free line to his unprotected knight.

I make my move.

About a minute later another message from Charles Dickens pops up.

Charles Dickens: *Damn, that's a good move. Are you sure you came up with it by yourself?*

ChessLover365: *Maybe pirate jokes are my energy source, and now I've tapped into the power to slaughter you in chess every time.*

Charles Dickens: *I always knew pirates would be my downfall.*

ChessLover365: *Got to go, looking forward to seeing your next move.*

Charles Dickens: *I'm looking forward to seeing it too.*

I snort as I log out of the app. Then I collect my pile of marking into a box so I can take it home with me. An exciting Friday night awaits.

My phone rings as I reach my car. I prop the box of marking between my hip and the car so I can answer it.

It's Jules.

"I need your help," she says.

"What's up?"

"I have two tickets to a charity wine auction tonight. I was going to write about it for my blog, but Kelsey just bailed on me."

"A charity wine auction is not really my thing," I hedge. "I can't even afford to buy a molecule of the wine they sell at those things."

"You don't have to bid on anything. Just keep me company. Come on, you can rip yourself away from Sam for one night, can't you?"

"Sam's actually got a work thing on."

"Awesome. You've got no excuse then."

"Okay, I'll go with you, but I want it noted what an amazing friend I am."

I can almost hear her rolling her eyes. "It's noted. I'll pay you back by being your maid of honor when you marry Sam."

She ends the call before I can respond.

Damn. Now she's brought the Sam dilemma back to the forefront of my mind.

I climb into my car, dump my box of marking on the front seat, then start its engine.

As I drive home, I try to work out why I'm so unsettled.

The Anonymous Hookup

Maybe it's because I can't help feeling this only has the potential for heartbreak. Sam and I wouldn't work as a couple; he's far too high-powered for me. A TV director whose star is ascending would surely want a more suitable long term partner than a high school English teacher.

I don't want to end things with him. I don't think I could physically bring myself to do that.

From now on, I've got to be more careful about guarding my heart.

When I get home, Jules messages me the details of the wine auction. It's being held at a yacht club and the dress code is black tie.

So I obediently pull out my one good suit from my closet. It's by Tom Ford. I haven't worn it since I broke up with Preston. He's the one who insisted I buy it, telling me it was an investment, that I needed to dress to impress.

It looks good, but then, for the price I paid for it, you'd expect it to.

Sure enough, Jules gives a wolf-whistle when I meet her outside the venue.

"You scrub up nice," she says.

"You're not looking too shabby yourself." I stand back to admire her red dress.

We walk in, and it's exactly how I'd expect a wine auction at a yacht club to be.

Lots of well-dressed people, waitstaff circulating with trays of canapes that look more like works of art than edible food.

"I'll get us drinks." Jules makes a beeline for the bar.

Not wanting to look stupid standing by myself, I start browsing some of the wine displayed on a long glass table to one side of the room. I try not to have an instant heart attack when I read the retail price list. Whoever eventually drinks this wine had better know their pungent from their woody flavor, or it'll be a hell of a waste.

"We really must stop running into each other like this," a sexy voice murmurs in my ear.

I recognize the voice, because it's the same voice that's murmured many sexy things into my ear recently.

My mouth is instantly in a smile as I turn around, because something about Sam always makes me smile. "What are you doing here?"

He quirks an eyebrow. "I'm about to ask you the same question."

"Jules needed a plus one at the last minute," I explain. "What about you? I thought you had a work thing." Discomfort stabs at my gut. He didn't lie to me, did he?

"This is my work thing." He nods over to the corner and I spot Claire among a whole other gaggle of people. "Apparently bidding on over-priced wine is considered bonding by some people."

"I don't imagine you're their ideal buyer," I say.

"No. I'll try to resist asking the auctioneer if they have any beer instead."

I laugh.

Sam's eyes skim down me. "You look incredible," he says simply.

I take in his dark pin-striped suit that he's paired with a black shirt. "So do you."

He sidles closer so he can whisper again. "Although I still prefer you naked."

"Right back at you," I say.

We grin at each other and warmth flushes through me.

I tear my gaze away, trying to regain control of my heart.

Unfortunately, as I look around the room, I spot another familiar face.

I'm not nearly as happy to see this particular face though.

My stomach sinks.

Preston.

Shit, I should have realized there was a good chance he'd be here. It's one of those mingling events he absolutely adores, a chance to be seen by the right people.

About a second after I spot him, he lifts his head and looks directly at me.

Then, like something out of a horror movie, he says something to his boss Kelly, and they detach from the group they're standing with and head in our direction.

And while I always liked Kelly, the idea of having to make small talk with Preston has my stomach churning.

"Can you pretend to be my boyfriend for a few minutes?" I whisper frantically to Sam as Preston and Kelly bear down on us.

Sam's eyebrows fly up. "Sure. I think I can do a great job of pretending to be your boyfriend." Something in his delivery is off. There's a flatness in his voice that isn't normally there.

But there isn't time for me to analyze it, because suddenly Preston and Kelly are right in front of us.

"Lane, so nice to see you." Kelly leans forward and gives me a kiss on my cheek.

"Nice to see you too," I say to her.

"Yes, good to see you." Preston's tone is cool.

"Hi Preston," I manage to get out.

Preston looks at Sam, who has moved to hover protectively at my side, then raises an eyebrow expectantly at me. Shit, just seeing that look on his face reminds me of all the times he decided I'd failed in these types of social situations. He'd berate me about it afterwards, telling me I needed to pay more attention to getting the minor details right, as that was what other people would judge me on.

"Oh, sorry, I should introduce you. This is my boyfriend, Sam," I say.

Preston's eyebrows continue their upward rise, threatening to leave his face entirely.

"Sam, this is Preston, and Preston's boss, Kelly. Preston and I dated for a while." I deliberately keep my words and tone casual. After all, Preston accused me of being clingy. I'm determined to show him I'm not a clingy ex.

A muscle in Preston's jaw ticks. "We were together three years."

"That sounds about right," I say easily.

Luckily Kelly offers a distraction. She's been staring at Sam with her forehead creased and suddenly her expression lifts. "Oh my god, you're Sam Heaney!"

Sam gives a charming smile. "I sure am."

"I'm a massive fan of *Getting the Goons*," Kelly gushes. "It's such a great show."

Preston's head jerks as he looks over at Sam.

"Thanks," Sam says smoothly. "It's always nice to meet a fan."

"That last episode, when they were in the school, was comic genius. I don't think I've ever laughed as hard," Kelly says.

Preston's eyes narrow.

"Actually, I'm planning to do a few more episodes set in the school next season," Sam says.

"Really?"

"Lane has really inspired me with all his teaching stories." Sam sends me a smile.

"So, you're just with me for my insights into teaching then," I say playfully.

He gives me a cute nose-scrunch in reply. "There are some other benefits too." He reaches out his arm and pulls me to him, depositing a kiss on the side of my head.

Preston makes a choking noise in the back of his throat. It sounds like some geese have gone there to die.

"And what do you do, Preston?" Sam asks.

Preston sends me a disbelieving look, like he can't believe I haven't told my new boyfriend about him.

"I'm an accountant," Preston says.

Sam gives a polite smile. "Oh, right."

"We're just boring money people," Kelly says. "I really admire anyone in the creative arts like you. Especially people who can make a career out of it."

"Thanks," Sam says easily.

Preston's shoulders stiffen. "I need to finish checking out the wine. Are either of you planning to bid on anything tonight?"

"I'm more of a beer drinker and I think I've tempted Lane over to the dark side," Sam says easily.

I look at him. "I've actually always preferred beer to wine."

When I glance back at Preston, he's frowning.

"Well, it was lovely to see you again, Lane." Kelly gives me another air kiss. "And wonderful to meet you, Sam."

"You too." Sam gives her a genuine smile, then flicks his gaze to Preston. "Nice to meet you."

Preston aims a stiff smile at both of us as he leaves.

Part of me is triumphant, because is there anything better than meeting your ex when you have a gorgeous, successful man standing next to you claiming to be your boyfriend? But there's a part of me that is sad too. I spent three years trying to be something I wasn't just to impress Preston. What a waste.

Sam and I are silent as we watch Preston and Kelley walk across to the wine presentation table.

"So, that's your ex," Sam says finally. His voice is quiet.

"Yeah, that's him."

"Did I do a good job pretending to be your boyfriend?" he asks. The hurt in his voice cuts at me, but it's nothing compared to the hurt I see on his face when my eyes snap up to meet his.

Because we both know there was no pretending involved. That it's exactly how Sam always acts toward me.

My stomach hollows.

"Sam —" I start. He holds up his hand to interrupt me, which is good, as I don't know how I'm planning to finish.

"No, Lane, don't apologize. You've always been upfront with me about what this is and isn't between us." He takes a deep breath, looking at the floor. "But I don't think I can keep on doing this with you."

"You're ending it?" Despite my best efforts, my voice wobbles.

I knew it. I knew Sam would realize he's too good for me.

My chest feels like it's been clamped in a vice.

"Yeah, I'm ending it." He raises his gaze to mine. "Because nothing is lonelier than falling in love with someone who's not in the same place."

I just stand there, stunned, as he walks away from me.

Sam.

Oh my god. Sam.

Sam claims he's falling in love with me?

Suddenly Jules is there offering me a glass of beer. I take it from her without thinking, my mind still struggling to grasp Sam's words.

He's falling in love with me?

"What just happened?" she asks. "I saw you and Sam talking to Preston. It was like watching a car crash when you can't look away."

I blink at her. Preston is the last thing on my mind right now.

Concern creases her forehead. "Are you okay?"

"Sam..." I whisper.

"What about him?"

"He ended it with me."

"What? Why? Are you absolutely sure? From the way he looked at you last night, I find that very hard to believe."

My lips feel numb but I manage to force the words out. "He said he's falling in love with me."

Her forehead scrunches. "What? He's ending it because he's falling in love with you? That makes absolutely no sense."

"He said he's ending it because he doesn't think I'm in the same place."

"Well, did you tell him you are?"

I don't reply.

"Oh my fucking god, Lane. What is wrong with you? Sam's like... insanely great."

"Exactly."

"What do you mean, exactly?"

"I mean, I couldn't keep Preston and he's a pretentious asshole. What chance do I have long-term with Sam, who is better looking and more successful than Preston, plus is the nicest guy on the planet?"

"I think you've answered your own question there."

My brow furrows. "What do you mean?"

"Sam's a nice guy. A really nice guy. He's not Preston."

"No, he's not, thank god."

I can't even begin to list the ways that Sam is not like

Preston. What we have together is so different from what I had with Preston.

So why do I still feel like I can't keep him long-term?

I preach to my students that no one can make you feel inferior without your consent, but do I actually apply it to myself?

Preston made me feel inferior. I let him get inside my head.

My job wasn't good enough. My clothes weren't good enough. My taste in wine wasn't good enough.

"You can't compare what happened with Preston with what potentially could happen with Sam because they're completely different people," Jules continues. "I can't imagine Sam ever belittling you in that condescending way like Preston used to do."

"No. Sam would never do that."

"I actually can't imagine him ever making you feel bad about yourself."

She's so right. There has never been a moment when we've been together that Sam has done or said anything to undermine me.

"Sam makes me laugh more than anyone I've ever met," I whisper. "And being with him... it's effortless, you know? I never realized how much effort I had to put into my relationship with Preston until I've had this with Sam."

"Why the hell are you telling all of this to me? I think there's someone else who needs to hear it."

Fear threatens to choke me as I imagine saying all of this to Sam.

Because when it boils down to it, I'm scared. I've tried desperately to keep things casual between Sam and me because I haven't wanted to get too attached, too invested in this thing growing between us.

And the more I've found out about Sam, the more I've been intimidated. He's smart. Funny. Talented.

It's been so much easier to just keep pretending we were just hooking up, that this wasn't the start of something.

The idea of going back to my life without Sam in it is awful. Because I would be giving up the best thing that's ever happened to me.

The realization slams into me and my breath leaves me in a gush.

Holy shit.

Jules is right. I need to tell him how I feel.

My throat feels tight as I scan the yacht club desperately. I finally spot him standing by the door to the bathroom. He's talking to Claire, his expression sombre. Claire reaches out to put a hand on his arm.

I move toward him through the crowd.

Even with his eyebrows pulled together and frowning, he's so incredibly gorgeous.

I swallow, but keep myself walking in a straight line.

Claire glances up and sees me. She says something to Sam and he twists to watch me approach. The look on his face is inscrutable.

Nerves crowd my stomach. I feel like I could throw up.

"Can we talk?" I ask.

Sam bites his lip. "Sure."

"On the deck?"

"Okay."

My shoulders are stiff as I turn and lead him outside.

Sam silently follows me through the French doors onto the deck. It overlooks the harbor, where row after row of shiny yachts are moored, bobbing under the stars.

When I turn to look at Sam, the vulnerable expression on his face slices through me. Suddenly, my own insecurities don't matter. Nothing matters but wiping that look off Sam's face.

"You said you were falling in love with me," I begin.

He scrapes his foot along the wood of the deck. "Yes, I am," he says quietly.

"Then you're right, we're not in the same place." I take a deep breath. "I'm already head over heels in love with you."

His gaze snaps up to mine.

"I'm so sorry. I've hidden behind the casual thing because I was scared of how fast and hard I was falling for you, but holy shit, Sam, what we have together is incredible."

He swallows, his Adam's apple bobbing as relief overtakes his face. "Yeah, it is. It really is."

He's been vulnerable with me tonight, and I owe it to him to be honest, so I push ahead with words from a deep, dark place inside of me. "And I guess I've been worried about whether this would work long-term because it feels like you're too good for me."

His eyebrows shoot up, surprise overtaking his face. "Are you kidding me, Lane? You're smart and kind and so much fun to be around. You're everything I've ever wanted in a man, wrapped up in a gorgeous package." His gaze doesn't leave mine, as if he's trying to convince me from the intensity of his stare alone the truth in his words. "And you have a gorgeous package as well, which is an added bonus."

I laugh. "Thanks."

"From the first moment in the bar when you told me you were thirsty, I've been so... captivated... by you." He runs his hand through his hair. "And every moment we've spent together has made me even more so. I've never fallen so hard and fast for anyone else before either, but I think... I think it just means it's the real deal."

"It feels like the real deal to me too," I say softly.

We stare at each other and then a slow smile spreads on his face. "So, you want to redefine this as an exclusive affair with lots of strings attached that never-ends?" he asks.

"There's another word for that I know of," I say.

Sam's dark eyes don't leave mine. "What's that?"

"Boyfriends."

Sam ducks his head for a moment. When he looks up, the grin on his face is the biggest I've ever seen. It's also completely contagious, and I feel a smile overtaking my face.

He moves forward to loop his arms around me, pulling me close. "I really, really like that definition," he says.

Then he kisses me.

Chapter Nine

I've always enjoyed waking up with Sam's arms around me, but the next morning it's at another level. Because this is waking up with my boyfriend, my boyfriend who I love and who claims he's falling in love with me too.

He lazily opens one eye, then closes it again.

"Are you staring at me like a stalker?" he asks sleepily.

"I don't think you can call me a stalker when I'm your boyfriend."

A smile comes over his lips. "True, those terms might be mutually exclusive." He pulls me tighter to him.

"Yeah, definitely." I lean forward to kiss him properly. And then we proceed to do the type of things that boyfriends like to do with each other.

Afterwards, we head to his house, taking Casper with us so the dogs can play together. I read on the couch while Sam putters around, cleaning up some clutter in his living room. When he puts away some magazines, he leaves one of the drawers under his coffee table open. From my position on the coach, I spy a familiar item.

I sit up straighter. "Is that a chessboard?"

He follows my gaze. "Yeah, my mum is a chess nut, so I couldn't avoid playing chess. Why? Do you play too?"

"Yeah, I play a bit," I say.

He squints appraisingly at me. "You want a game?"

"Depends. How much do you feel like losing?"

"Oh, we're bringing the smack talk about chess, are we?" Sam is already setting up the board on the coffee table.

"Chess isn't fun without smack talk," I inform him, shuffling myself forward on the couch so I can reach the white pieces.

I make my opening move, and Sam counters it. My chest feels like it's filled with helium. I can't believe this is another thing we share.

It's only when we're five moves in that I realize there's something very familiar with the moves Sam is pulling out.

I stare at the board. It's Charles Dickens's signature opening sequence. The one he uses every time we play.

My breath leaves me in a whoosh.

No way. No way.

Sam sends me a confused look.

Our lives are already so intertwined. Surely this can't be another place where they intersect?

Maybe it's just a coincidence? My face feels tingly as my breathing rate increases.

"Your move," I say.

If he moves his bishop to threaten my queen, then it can't just be coincidence.

He picks up his bishop and my breath hitches.

"Knock knock," a loud voice calls as Sam's front door creaks opens.

Alarm spreads on Sam's face. "Please tell me you'll still love me after this."

I blink. "Wait. What?"

Before he can answer, the door opens fully and a woman bursts in. She looks to be in her late forties and has fiery red hair with a streak of purple running through the middle.

"My son!" she says dramatically as she comes across the living room and throws her arms around Sam.

Despite the nerves clamping my stomach, I grin. So, that solves the mystery of where Sam got his theatrical side.

"Hi Mum," Sam's voice is halfway between affectionate and resigned.

She lets go of Sam and pivots to face me. "And who do we have here?" Her voice is layered with expectation.

"This is Lane, my boyfriend. Lane, this is my mother Alice."

His mother's eyebrows shoot up.

"Nice to meet you," I say, offering my hand.

She shakes it, her gaze narrowing in suspicion.

"Since when do you have a boyfriend?" she asks Sam as she drops my hand, her voice somewhere between hurt and accusing.

"We made it official last night," Sam says.

My heart thuds as her eyes swivel back to me. Shit. I don't think I've ever been on the receiving end of such a penetrating stare. It's like she's trying to see into my soul and uncover all my secrets. From everything Sam's told me about her, I'm guessing she's going to be intense when it comes to vetting the boyfriend of her precious only child.

When she drops my hand, I run a hand through my hair, which I haven't bothered to comb after our shower together. Damn.

"We were just playing a game of chess," Sam says. I'm

not sure if it's an attempt to distract her away from scrutinizing me.

She squints down at the chessboard. "Ha, you're doing my opening sequence. I taught you well."

Her opening sequence?

My mind spins and a fluttery feeling begins in my stomach.

What the hell?

"Yeah, well, I haven't played for a while, so copying your moves is the best I could do under pressure," Sam informs her.

"I'm actually very familiar with this opening," I say slowly. "Were you about to move your bishop to threaten my queen?"

Sam and his mother's forehead both scrunch identically. It's adorable.

"How do you know that?" Sam asks.

But it's not Sam I look at. Instead, I look at Alice. "It's been said Jedi mind tricks don't work on me because I have no mind. However, I do know Charles Dickens's middle names, and I always appreciate a good pirate joke."

Her mouth drops open and for a few moments she just gapes at me. I get the feeling that rendering Alice speechless is somewhat of an achievement.

"ChessLover365?" she finally manages.

I give her my best grin. "I have been known to respond to that name."

She tips her head back and roars with laughter.

Sam's gaze ping-pongs between us, confusion stamped on his face. "What the hell is happening here?"

Alice and I continue to laugh.

Finally Alice wipes away a tear of laughter. "Oh Sammy, you've found a good one," she says happily.

Sam's eyebrows threaten to fly off his head. "What? Can one of you please explain?"

I decide to put him out of his misery. "Your mother and I have been playing chess online against each other for three years."

He blinks at me. Then blinks some more.

"You've got to be kidding me," he says finally.

Alice throws a smirk in my direction. "If you saw some of his moves, you'd definitely think there's a joke in there somewhere."

* * *

Alice stays for half an hour, chatting with Sam and me, all of us continuing to marvel at the incredible coincidence.

"So, that was beyond surreal," Sam says after she leaves. He still looks shell-shocked.

"Ah...yeah."

My phone beeps with a message. I have a sneaking suspicion I know who it's from.

Charles Dickens: *What are your intentions with my son???*

I grin as I type out a reply.

Chesslover365: *Have lots of great sex with him.*

Charles Dickens: *Okay. I probably deserved that mental scarring you just provided.*

Chesslover365: *And my work here is done.*

"Your mum's a riot," I say as I flash him the message.

Sam takes my phone from me and scrolls through a few months' worth of the banter and insults that have flown between me and his mother. He swallows hard before he raises his eyes to me.

"And I thought you couldn't be any more perfect," he says.

"I'm perfect because I trash talk your mother?"

He sits back, a happy smile spreading over his face. "Normally I'm extremely worried about how my boyfriends will handle her. But I get the feeling you can hold your own just fine."

"It helps I've had a few years of training," I say.

He picks up one of the chess pieces and turns it over in his hand, his face contemplative. "It's so crazy, it's like... you were hovering in the background of my life all of this time. Our dogs have been playing together for months. You'd applied for your students to do a mentorship with my work and you'd been emailing one of my best friends. My mother has been playing online chess against you for THREE years. And then one night, you just walk into a club and proposition me..." He shakes his head.

"There are some incredible coincidences," I agree.

He sets the chess piece back on the board before he looks up, his dark eyes capturing mine. "Or there is another word to describe it."

"What's that?" I say.

"Fate."

I can't hide my smile at that thought.

His eyes stay intense on mine as he continues, "Even if that night hadn't happened, we would have met at doggie daycare, and then again at the studio. I like to think we would've eventually arrived at the same place."

"I love that idea," I say quietly.

It's an extremely appealing concept that the universe did everything it could to throw us together, that we were destined to find our way to each other regardless of how it happened.

"Although, I think we're going to have to decide whether we go with doggie daycare, me tutoring your students, or you playing chess against my mother."

I screw up my face in confusion. "What do you mean?"

Sam just gives me a cheeky grin, although his eyes are full of love. "Well, we're going to need a better official story about how we met for when the kids come along, aren't we?"

Epilogue

One year later

"Mr F, Mr F. Sir! Over here!" The moment we enter the auditorium Rosa bounces up and down in her seat in the front row, indicating the free seats next to her.

I lift my hand to acknowledge her before turning to Sam. "Are you happy to sit with my students? It looks like they've saved us space in the front row."

Sam's eyebrows draw together. "That's fine," he says. "Closer to the podium for me, I guess."

Sam has been uncharacteristically quiet the entire way here. Maybe he's nervous about having to introduce my students' show? I can't imagine his nerves are about the show itself. He and my students came up with a comedic murder mystery and the whole thing is supremely awesome. Not that I'm biased, of course.

I send a sideways glance at him. He didn't even seem

this nervous before the TV awards a few months ago, when *Getting the Goons* scooped up the major prize and he had to give an acceptance speech in front of the television cameras and the 'Who's Who' of the New Zealand entertainment industry.

That success propelled Sam into a whole other level of fame, to the point where people now recognize him wherever we go.

But I've never had a moment of insecurity from being in a relationship with someone so well known. We're so happy together, our relationship so strong, that I can never doubt us.

Instead, I'm just glad the entire country now realizes how awesome he is.

I grab his hand and give it a reassuring squeeze.

Sam blows out a breath and gives me a shaky smile.

I don't have time to ask him if he's okay, because we've reached the front row and are surrounded by students.

"Mr Fenwick!" Tabitha is basically bouncing up and down on the spot.

"Can't believe we have to wear uniform," Viliami moans, tugging at the collar of his blazer. It's the continuation of his complaints from school when he discovered they'd be wearing the dress uniform to the event tonight.

"You are representing the school," I remind him.

"Hi, Sir's boyfriend," Rosa greets Sam with a smirk.

She'd taken to calling him that after my students discovered we were dating. We'd done a good job of hiding it for the first few months at the studio, but it came out one day when Sam had given me a slightly too affectionate look after I'd made a Sherlock Holmes joke, and when he'd left the room, Rosa had turned to me. "I think Sam Heaney's got a crush on you, Sir."

Tobias, of all people, had rolled his eyes at her. "Duh. They're boyfriends. Haven't you worked that out?"

"What?" Rosa turned to stare at Tobias, and then back at me. "Is that true?"

"I don't comment on my personal life," I'd said, trying not to blush.

"Shit, that's not a denial," Rosa said.

"Language," I warned.

Sam came back into the room. Rosa narrowed her eyes. "You might not comment on your love life, but Mr Heaney can," she said, marching straight over to Sam. "Are you Sir's boyfriend?"

A grin lit up Sam's face and he looked over at me. "Have they found us out?"

"I've neither confirmed nor denied," I said with a smile.

"Oh my god, it's true!!" Rosa whirled around to face me. "Way to go Sir!"

"Ah... thanks," I said.

Rosa turned her attention to Tobias. "How did you know?" She looked slightly affronted he'd known something she hadn't.

"Last week, Mr Heaney wore Mr Fenwick's tie with the Shakespeare quotes on it," he said.

Shit. He'd been right. Sam stayed the night at my place and had been running late the next morning when he realized he had a meeting with the show's sponsors and needed a tie, so I'd loaned him one of mine.

"I could have had my own Shakespeare tie," Sam protested.

"Like you'd be cool enough to own a Shakespeare tie," I said.

"Hey, I can quote Shakespeare with the best of them." He'd grinned at me and we'd shared a smile.

"Ew yuck, now you're making gooey eyes at each other. That's gross," Rosa informed us.

So, for the sake of my students, Sam and I had tried to keep our gooey eyes just between us from then on.

The tie borrowing ceased a few months later, because when my house sitting stint ended, it had seemed a no-brainer for me to move into Sam's house so we could live together.

When my parents had come to Auckland and dropped in to visit me and meet Sam just after I moved in, Sam had been his usual charming self. And there had been something eternally satisfying seeing them realize that their quiet, overlooked fifth child had somehow found a career he loved and also had an incredibly handsome and successful partner.

I'd occasionally had a pinch myself moment, as we'd worked in the garden together or relaxed at the end of the day on the outdoor lounge suite of the newly constructed deck, drinking beer and talking and laughing and kissing... lots of kissing.

Talking about pinch yourself moments, it looks like I'm about to have another one as I spot a familiar face coming into the auditorium.

Jules.

She's making a beeline for the stairs, but I'm on my feet and intercept her before she reaches them.

"What are you doing here?" I ask.

Jules flicks a look at Sam who's now sitting in the front row. She looks almost...guilty.

"I wanted to see your students' show," she says.

My forehead furrows

But the theatre lights are darkening, so I don't have a

chance to talk to her further as she scurries off to find a seat a few rows back.

I sit down next to Sam.

Claire takes the podium first, looking elegant in a deep blue dress as she talks through the aims of the program.

Then one of the other directors stands up to introduce the show her students produced and we settle back to watch the half hour episode.

Call me biased, but it's not a patch on the show Sam and my students have put together.

The next director talks and we watch another show, before finally, it's Sam's turn to introduce Southlake's show.

I sit up straighter. Sam looks so handsome and confident standing at the podium and I feel a rush of pride flow through me. Sometimes I still can't believe he's mine.

"Hi everyone, I'm Sam Heaney and it was my absolute privilege to work with the students from Southlake High on the show you're about to watch. I've learned a lot from them and I hope they've managed to learn a few things from me too. So, without further ado, I present to you 'The Onehunga Murder Files.'"

He smiles at the light applause and then heads back to sit next to me.

"You did great," I murmur to him.

He gives me a smile but there's still a stressed out element to it.

Sam's remains twitchy throughout the show. I put my hand on his thigh to settle him. I don't know what he's so worried about. The show is an absolute hit. The audience laughs and flinches in all the right places.

At the end the applause is deafening. I grin as I clap so hard I'm at risk of dislocating my wrists.

I turn to say something to Sam, but he's not in his seat anymore. Instead, he's halfway back to the podium.

My forehead scrunches. What is he doing?

He leans down to speak into the microphone. "Before we conclude for the evening, the Southlake students and I have a bonus scene we want to share with you."

What the hell? I frown. What extra scene? I don't know anything about an extra scene.

Sam nods at the guy in the lighting and sound box and suddenly Rosa's on the screen, looking like a Pacific Island princess with her hair in complex braids, holding a piece of paper that she reads from.

"This is a quote from Anna Karenina," she says as she lifts her eyes to the camera. "I've always loved you, and when you love someone, you love the whole person, just as he or she is, and not as you would like them to be."

I smile, because that's always been one of my favorite quotes from the classics.

Next, Viliami's face pops up, grinning his cheeky grin.

"Love is when two people know everything about each other and are still friends. Mark Twain."

It's another quote I love.

When did they film this? It must have been a few weeks ago when I was sick with the flu. Sam had been so sweet while I was sick, finding me Netflix shows to binge watch, bringing me endless lemon and honey drinks.

It's Elroy's turn next. And then Tabitha's.

It's cute seeing my students read classic love quotes from literature. Especially knowing I'd get epic eye rolls if I tried to introduce any of these works in class.

Tobias is the last student to speak. "You don't love someone for their looks, or their clothes, or for their fancy

The Anonymous Hookup

car, but because they sing a song only you can hear. Oscar Wilde."

Oh my god. I had that quote on my wall at university.

My heart is now beating loudly in my ears.

But the clip hasn't finished yet.

Alice's face fills the screen, with her unmistakable red hair and streak of purple.

What the everlasting hell?

I blink, but the image remains. Sam's mother is in a video with my students.

How? Why?

"This quote is from Charles Dickens," she says, her characteristic grin lighting up her face. "In case you ever foolishly forget, I am never not thinking of you."

I can't breathe because my chest feels like a giant has picked me up to give me a good squeeze.

But the surprises don't stop coming.

When Alice fades out, Jules is on the screen.

I whip my head around to stare at the real Jules.

She grins, then gives me a pointed nod, directing my attention back to the video.

The on-screen version of Jules is reading my favorite Emily Bronte quote. "He's more myself than I am. Whatever our souls are made of, his and mine are the same."

Then Sam's handsome face fills the screen.

My face feels all tingly and my breath comes in short gasps as he grins. Sam smiling has to be my favorite sight in the world. "In the words of Shakespeare, 'I would not wish any companion in the world but you'."

My eyes are still focused on screen Sam when I realize real Sam has made his way back from the podium and is right in front of me.

He's down on one knee and my vision blurs and my

chest heaves, but I wipe my eyes so I can see his face and the ring he's holding in the palm of his hand.

I choke back a sob.

His eyes don't leave mine, his dark eyes as earnest as I've ever seen them.

"Lane Fenwick," he says. "I, Sam Heaney, want nothing more than to spend the rest of my life with you, talking with you, laughing with you, running with you, practicing the art of hydration with you…"

I huff out a wet laugh.

"Will you please do me the honor of becoming my husband?" he asks.

"Oh my god, Sam," I manage.

He tilts his head, his eyes still not leaving mine. "Is that a yes?"

"Of course it's a yes."

As he leans forward to kiss me the whole auditorium bursts into loud applause that fills my ears, matching the incredibly full feeling inside my chest as Sam's warm lips press against mine.

Afterwards, my head is spinning as crowds of people engulf Sam and me to congratulate us.

My students are almost delirious about the part they got to play in our engagement story.

"It's like one of the scenes we did for our audition video, only better," Tabitha says.

"I still think he should have proposed pretending to be Aquaman with the ring on a trident. That would have been so sick," Elroy says.

I laugh and run my fingertips over the shiny platinum of the ring on my finger.

"Congratulations!" a voice I didn't expect says in my ear.

I whirl around. Alice.

How did she sneak in here without me seeing? All my questions flee though, as she engulfs me in the most bone-crushing hug. When she pulls back her eyes are glistening. "I can't believe I get another son!"

"Why do I feel like that message should come with its own ominous soundtrack?" I quip and she laughs loudly. Yup. I love Alice, and the feeling appears to be mutual.

Jules approaches me then and she and Alice do a bit of mutual appreciation for their part in the subterfuge before Alice heads off toward Sam.

"You know, you never wrote that post for my blog," Jules says to me.

"It'll need a major title revision now," I say.

She snorts. "What, you don't think 'How to have an anonymous hookup' applies anymore?"

"Ah no. Not really. Maybe more like 'How to meet your soul mate and be deliriously happy for the rest of your life'?"

Jules rolls her eyes. "Like I'd ever let something that sappy onto my blog."

I laugh.

"So, do I get a thank you?" she asks.

"What for?"

"Well, it was my idea for you to have an anonymous hookup, right? And look how well that turned out for you."

I glance at Sam, who is chatting with his mother and Claire, everyone with enormous grins on their faces. Sam, my fiancé. Sam, who I get to spend the rest of my life with.

"It turned out pretty well," I agree with a smile.

"I think the take-home message here is very clear," Jules says.

"What's that?"

She smiles triumphantly. "You should always listen to me."

* * *

A note from Jax:

Thank you so much for reading! I really hope you enjoyed Sam and Lane's story. This novella originally started as a short story I was writing to cheer myself up, and just kept growing and growing from there!

I write lots of short stories and bonus scenes exclusively for my newsletter subscribers – you can sign up on my website www.jaxcalder.com/newsletter-sign-up or via Bookfunnel. When you sign up you'll receive my short novella *Being Set Up*, where Michael resists his well-meaning friends attempts to set him up, only to discover he might have just turned down the best thing to ever happen to him.

As a new author, reviews mean so much to me. If you have a chance, please consider leaving a review for this story. You can review this book on Amazon, Goodreads and BookBub.

Also by Jax Calder

Playing Offside: A M/M enemies to lovers sports romance

Aiden Jones, aka the Ice King, is one of the best rugby players in the world. And he's not about to surrender his starting spot in the New Zealand squad to Tyler Bannings, the cocky loudmouth who just joined the training squad. But when they end up rooming together at training camp, the heat between them threatens to melt even the Ice King. Now Aiden's falling for the same guy who's plotting to take his spot. But all's fair in love and sport, right?

Read on Kindle Unlimited or Buy NOW

Playing at Home: a M/M manny romance

Jacob Browne comes from rugby royalty but he's never lived up to being the heroic idol his father was on the rugby field. And now he's failed off the field as well with the breakdown of his marriage. When his ex-wife hires a manny, it feels like the ultimate kick in the guts that another guy gets to spend more time with his kids than he does.

But when he actually meets Austin, the connection that grows between them upends everything Jacob thought he knew about himself and forces him to reconsider what it truly means to be a hero.

Read on Kindle Unlimited or Buy NOW

Playing for Keeps: A friends-to-lovers sports romance

Falling for your former best friend? Never a good idea.

Luke Hunter has returned to New Zealand, determined to make the national team. So what if one of his new teammates is the person who shredded his heart? Luke's moved past that, and he's happy now. There is no way he's falling back under Ethan's spell.

But it turns out no matter how good you are at evading the opposition, there's one thing you can never escape—and that's the love of your life.

Pre-order NOW

The Other Brother: a YA/New Adult M/M romance

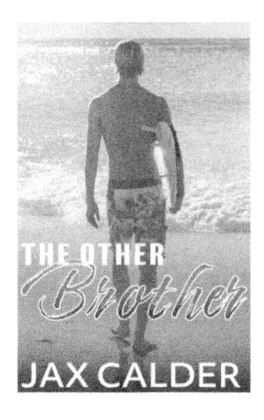

Ryan has had seventeen years of being compared to Cody, part of his toxic fractured family, so you'll forgive him for some epic eye-rolling when it comes to Mr Perfect. Although not related to him by blood, Cody has always been annoying background noise in Ryan's life.

One summer changes everything. It's the summer when circumstances collide, and they end up spending time together at Cody's family's beach house. It's the summer they become friends. And then more than friends.

But when summer ends, Cody and Ryan are forced back to reality. Can their relationship survive?

Read on Kindle Unlimited or Buy NOW

The Inappropriate Date: a heart-warming short M/M novella

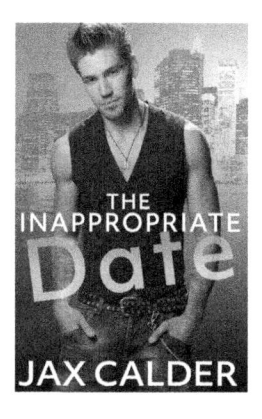

Hunter has always been a good son. Unfortunately, his mother struggles to handle the fact he's bisexual. When she warns him not to bring someone inappropriate to his sister's wedding, Hunter decides to find the most inappropriate date possible.

Blue Hair. Tattoos. Most definitely male. There's more chance his mother will learn to moonwalk than approve of Adam as his date. But appearances can be deceiving. And Hunter is about to learn this lesson along with the rest of his family...

Read on Kindle Unlimited or Buy NOW

About the Author

Jax's stories are all about light-hearted conversations and deeply-felt connections. She lives in New Zealand with her family and a wide assortment of animals. She's a rabid sports fan, a hiking enthusiast and has a slightly unhealthy addiction to nature documentaries. She is also a massive fan of M/M romance and enjoys both reading and writing it.

Jax is an extrovert living a writers' introverted life where she spends WAY too much time in her own head, so she'd love to hear from you in whatever way you want to connect with her:

You can hang out on Facebook in her authors group Jax's Crew...

https://www.facebook.com/groups/jaxcaldercrew/

Or follow her on Facebook, Instagram, BookBub or Goodreads

And don't forget to sign up to her newsletter via BookFunnel or her website www.jaxcalder.com/newsletter

Also, feel free to email her at any time, she'll always respond: jax@jaxcalder.com

Printed in Great Britain
by Amazon